Rescue Me

by

Jody Vitek

Published by
Melange Books, LLC
White Bear Lake, MN 55110
www.melange-books.com

ISBN: 978-1-61235-696-9 Print

Cover Art by Caroline Andrus

Rescue Me
Jody Vitek

Can Catherine accept the consequences of a great-aunt's dying wish without losing her heart or independence?

Taking in stray, injured or needy animals, veterinarian doctor Catherine Mornelli opens the Four Hooves and Paws Rescue program. But the land where the animals are kept is being sold. She approaches her Great-Aunt Elaine about possibly using her barn. However, visiting her aunt and checking out the barn also means seeing her ex-boyfriend.

Josef Garrison farms land that once belonged to his family for generations but went to his neighbor Elaine after his great-grandfather lost it in a poker game to Catherine's great-grandfather. When Catherine returns, he sees a way to win back her heart and the land at the same time.

Dedication

I must give thanks to my loving mom Margaret for taking my brother and me to "the farm" during the summer months when we were kids. Big thanks to my Great-Aunt Eleanor Madison and her family for entertaining us during our visits there. This book wouldn't exist without these wonderful memories.

* * * *

Acknowledgements

To my fabulous critique partners: Joyce, Terri, Cathleen and Brenda. You helped make this book complete. And I can't forget to thank my wonderful editor Jane for working with me again.

Chapter One

"Aunt Elaine, how are you?" Catherine Mornelli twisted a section of her black hair around a finger as she sat at her workspace. Elaine, her great-aunt, had something she could use. Money was tight, what with paying off student loans and her own living expenses. And she had the expenses of her rescue operation.

"Catherine, what a pleasant surprise. Is everything okay?" The concern in her aunt's voice couldn't be missed.

"Fine. Nothing to worry about," Catherine assured her. "I have a question, or better yet, a favor to ask of you." Two weeks ago, she had started the search to locate a new home for her rescue horses. Their current location in Pinedale, Minnesota was up for sale.

"Anything for you, dear. You know that."

Sincerity sounded in Elaine's voice and filled Catherine's chest with warmth. "Are you using your barn?"

"No. I have no use for that thing. Although, Joe's using the hayloft for storage."

"Okay, that shouldn't be a problem." Her love for animals stemmed from the summer months spent on the farm throughout her younger years.

"What do you need a barn for? Is this for the horses your mother's been telling me about?" Aunt Elaine's excitement traveled through the phone line, and although Catherine wasn't in front of her, she envisioned her aunt's dentured smile and crinkled eyes, hiding behind large plastic framed glasses.

"That's exactly the reason. The place where I'm now boarding the

1

horses is for sale, and I don't know how long I have until it sells. I've been looking around and then thought of you." Property sold quickly in the southern suburbs of Saint Paul and Minneapolis. Housing sprawled out and popped up in place of farmland.

"Consider it yours." No hesitation.

Exhilarated, her heart beat like a horse jumping a combination— pole after pole after pole. Relief washed over tense shoulders, and she released the strand of twisted hair. "Great! I'm going to plan a trip up to see you. I want to take a look at the barn."

"I'll get the room ready for you. Joe was over today." The last bit of information rolled off her aunt's tongue slow but dangerous like a steamroller.

"Really?" The word escaped her lips in a more snotty tone than intended. She wasn't interested in Josef despite what her aunt might think. He was a part of her past.

"He comes to visit every now and then to check on me and see if I need any help."

"Huh." Disinterested in hearing about Josef, Catherine perused the papers sitting on the desk.

"He looked at my water heater."

"I was hoping this weekend would work for you." She changed the ex-boyfriend topic. Although he was history, her memory brought forth a picture of him, twenty-one with shaggy black hair and brown caring eyes.

"That'd be fine, Catherine. I'll see you Saturday."

"Actually, I was planning on being there Friday night. Will that work for you?"

"Of course. Will you be here for dinner? I could see if Joe's available."

"Sorry, no. I have to work and then go home before hitting the road."

"That's too bad."

"I'll see him while I'm there, Aunt Elaine," she said to satisfy the woman's pushing about Josef. When Catherine and Josef ended their relationship eleven years ago, it pained her aunt. Elaine had big plans for the two of them and was never afraid to voice them.

"I'm sure you will. Now don't forget to pack your Sunday clothes. Mass is at nine o'clock."

"Dr. Mornelli, you're needed in Room Two-D stat," her assistant rattled at her while Elaine spoke of church. "Someone brought in a dog that was hit by a car."

Catherine put a finger up in acknowledgement and shook her head. "Aunt Elaine, I've got to go. We have an emergency here at the clinic. See you Friday night."

Not giving her aunt a chance to say goodbye, she hung up and hustled to Room Two-D.

"The man who brought the dog in said he couldn't avoid hitting him," the assistant informed her. "He saw a car clip the dog, which flung the animal into the front side of his truck. He pulled over and loaded the dog into the back of his pickup."

"What kind of dog?" Catherine asked.

"Appears to be a mix. Big. One-forty."

They stepped into the room, and a remorseful-looking man paced the small confines of the exam room.

"Sir, do you know whose dog this is?" Catherine inquired, approaching the dog lying on the exam table.

"No. I was driving and ... I'm so sorry." Sorrow etched his face.

"There's no need to be sorry. You've done the right thing by bringing him here." With tender fingers, she examined the dog. As she touched his hind leg, he yelped.

"Can you help him even if he's not mine?" The man's voice quavered.

"Yes. We'll take great care of him." The dog's back right hindquarter had lacerations, and the leg appeared to be broken. "Sir, if you wouldn't mind stepping from the room, we need to take care of this big fella. The receptionist will talk to you."

"Okay." Visibly distraught, the man left. Catherine knew the staff would reassure him about the dog's well-being.

The room cleared, she ordered an x-ray for confirmation and to catch anything she couldn't see. The surgery room was sterile and cool. Goose bumps congregated on her arms regardless of the long sleeves covering them. Catherine didn't like music played in the operating room while working on a patient. The barking, squawking, and other animal vocalization in the background was her soundtrack. *They* were the driving purpose of her life's work.

"What's the chance of the dog making it, Catherine?" Her assistant asked once surgery was completed.

"He should make a full recovery." Catherine walked through the operating room doors and removed her surgical gloves, disposing of them into the hazard bin. "But like every surgery, we'll have to wait and see."

"Are you paying for this one?"

"I'll cover the costs. You know me." She untied and removed her gown, tossing it into the laundry hamper. Un-owned animals brought into the clinic were a rarity. In cases like this though, Catherine couldn't help but treat and take care of the animal.

"Are you going to take him in, too?" The assistant removed her gown and turned toward the operating area where other assistants finished cleaning the dog and room.

"I can't save him to leave him without a home. He doesn't have a microchip, so we'll wait to see if he has an owner. If no owner shows up in a week, I'll take him home with me until we can find him a place." Catherine sat at her desk. "It's been a long day. Let's finish things so we can leave."

"Sounds good. Any plans for tonight?"

"I need to run to the farm and take care of the horses."

"The girls and I are going out for drinks. Why don't you join us?"

"Thanks, but I'll pass. You have fun." Girl's night out *would* be nice, but the horses came first. She could hook up with her friends later. But not tonight.

"Fun? Oh, we will." The assistant wriggled her eyebrows before going to the front office.

Catherine filled out the necessary paperwork for the surgery and, before leaving, checked on the patient.

"How you doing, big guy?" She squatted to the floor and looked in the cage. He appeared to be a Newfoundland mix. "I think I'll call you Fritz." His eyes opened enough to show off his beautiful brown irises, and he whined.

The dog sniffed the hand she placed in front of the cage, but kept his head still, eyes fixed on her.

"I'll check on you tomorrow morning. You'll be off your feet for a while." She stood, peering through the top of the enclosure at his hindquarter. Minor blood soaked through the bandage. After being struck by multiple cars, he was lucky to survive.

Saying good night to the remaining staff before leaving, she hopped into her silver pickup and made the twenty-minute drive to her townhouse. If Fritz moved in and joined the furry family, she would be over the limit of two animals per unit. There was a possibility of a fine by the city if caught, but a risk worth taking—the cats added to the dog count. It worked to her advantage to have the cats remain indoors. No one could see them, unless spotted sitting in a window.

She opened the door leading from the garage to the house. "Hey, Fuzzy." She picked the dog up and nuzzled her face into his black and white fluffy fur. Fuzzy was the first dog she adopted from a shelter when she started working at Lake View Animal Clinic. A puppy then, he had grown and dealt with her schedule and the animals she brought home. He was a true companion.

A paw touched her thigh. "Well hello, Darby," she said, acknowledging the yellow lab. "Give Mom a chance to change clothes, and I'll let you out."

In the bedroom, she pulled on jeans and a different shirt. "Hello, Mr. T. Where's your counterpart?" she questioned the black and white longhaired cat. A meow and rub on the shin, she picked up the multicolored calico cat and gave her a little loving. "Buddy, where have you been hiding?" The cat jumped to the bed, and Catherine left the cats to themselves.

"Come on, boys. Let's go out." Through the open sliding door, she clipped the dogs to their chains.

She ate a quick ham sandwich with chips and fruit before letting the dogs back inside. She tugged on Army green barn boots, grabbed the keys and held the door to the garage open. "Come on, guys. Let's go."

The dogs barked, and tails wagged. She opened the door to the pickup and waited for the "boys" to jump in the back of the cab.

Catherine drove south on I-35 headed for the farm where she

boarded the four rescue horses. Pinedale was a forty-five-minute drive from her place. She decelerated approaching the driveway to the farm. The real estate sign was a massive commercial size, not the small reality yard sign you normally saw. You could probably see this one from space.

She parked close to the barn and let Fuzzy and Darby loose to tear around the open space. The owner's dog, Rufus, joined the ruckus.

She unlatched the white barn door with black trim and greeted the horses—Steel, Rusty, Magnolia and Churchill—before leading them to pasture. Pitchfork, shovel and wheelbarrow ready to clean the stalls, she welcomed the distracting pungent smell of the manure as it stung her eyes and nostrils. She worked days at the clinic and cared for the horses at night. Locating a new place for them took time. Time she didn't have.

"Catherine," Warren's voice came from behind as she worked to clean the last stall. "Any luck with finding a new boarding facility?" the sixty-two year old asked with heartfelt sadness.

Warren, the current owner of the property and a widower, made the decision to put the property up for sale a month ago. Whenever Catherine couldn't make the trip to the farm, he helped care for the horses since he no longer had farm animals of his own.

"I might've. I'm going to my aunt's this weekend to check the condition of her barn. Will you be around to help with the horses, or should I find someone else?"

"I'll be around. I'm not going anywhere." He reached out and gave Rusty, who waited at the fence line, a pat on the neck and ran his hand down the horse's back. "Where's your aunt's place?"

"North. Oak City." She continued to shovel muck from the stall into the wheelbarrow. "I'm not sure though. With the drive, I may have to move and find a new job." She turned to face Warren. "This place will sell quickly, and I want a good handle on things before it does." She rested the shovel against the wall, grabbed the wheelbarrow handles and exited the barn.

He followed.

"I'll figure it out. Thanks, Warren." The manure and used shavings were added to the heap beyond the barn along the tree line.

"You're doing a good thing for these animals, Catherine. I hope the barn works out."

"Me, too." She pushed the wheelbarrow into the barn and spread fresh wood shavings in the stalls before leading the horses back in. "Keep me posted, and let me know if you sell."

"I'm sorry for putting it up for sale, Catherine." He wandered toward the barn doors.

"You need to quit apologizing, Warren. The time's come for you to move on with your life. You've been such a great help to me and the horses. I'll never forget that." Tears stung, and she wiped them away. "Damn manure."

Chapter Two

The Minnesota heat in June was unbearable to most, but Catherine didn't mind. Fresh evening air blew through the truck windows as she drove from the Twin Cities to the farm. The breeze cooled her sun-warmed skin while dancing the Tango with her fine hair.

It was a nice drive from the cities to the north. Leaving the tall office buildings of Minneapolis—St. Paul. Finding the smaller buildings of the suburban sprawl. Discovering the wide-open fields of varying crops. The atmosphere may have had an unpleasant odor to some as they drove past the fields, but she welcomed the clean air, not city smog. The further north one traveled the better the quality of air.

She exited the freeway and drove to the back dirt road that would take her to the farm. Large irrigation sprinklers moistened the parched soil. Not having had any rain and with none in the forecast, the farmers helped their crops along, otherwise they risked losing them.

The smell of manure and dust kicked up by the tires of her pickup on the gravel road brought on childhood memories. Ten years old again, she was experiencing the excitement of visiting her great-aunt and uncle's farm. To run free through the fields and play in the hayloft. Play on the swing hanging from the big oak tree, chase the chickens around the yard and, of course, help with the daily chores.

She shared the chores with the foster kids that came and went from Elaine and Gordon's farm. The foster kids would move to permanent homes sometimes leaving Catherine alone with her elderly kin. Since her Uncle Gordon's death ten years ago, her Aunt Elaine lived there alone.

The orange glow of the sun fell below the tree line. Without a need for sunglasses, she tossed hers on the dash. She slowed when she spotted Josef's mailbox on the right side of the road. A truck sat parked in his driveway sixty some feet away from the road. "Damn, he's home."

Fuzzy and Darby perked up from their slumber and poked their noses from the back of the truck's cab to the front seat.

"I don't see him, though." She drove a few yards, turned left onto Elaine's driveway and looked around. "It's just as I remember." The old school bus remained where she had last seen it. The old rusted farm equipment was parked in the out building, which also contained a shiny new looking green machine. The house was what she liked to call farmhouse white with black trim. The red barn's color had weathered over the years, but appeared good and sturdy.

Josef and Elaine sat on lawn chairs under the oak tree in the grassy center of the roundabout drive. They stood as the truck approached. Catherine groaned at the sight of the two. Her aunt was up to her old tricks, trying to get Josef and her back together.

"Shit." She brought the truck to a halt. "I should've known Aunt Elaine'd do something like this. Let's get your leashes on. I can't have you running off," she said to the dogs as she clipped the chains to their collars. "Okay, out." She opened the door, and they bounded from the truck.

The dogs pulled her forward. "Aunt Elaine, how are you? You look great." Catherine embraced her short round aunt who wore a large floral print dress. She whispered in the older woman's ear, "You planned this. Him being here."

"Nonsense," her aunt murmured before speaking louder. "I'm doing well."

"Josef, hard to believe you've gotten taller since ... well, years past." He wasn't the young college kid she remembered. He'd grown several inches, and his muscles were bulkier and well formed—all around.

"Cat. You've changed, too." He rubbed the dogs' heads, giving them the attention they sought from him. "What are their names?"

The dogs were enjoying the new environment and explored as far as the leashes allowed. "Fuzzy is the little guy, and Darby's the yellow lab." She forcefully twisted the tie-down stakes into the dry hard ground away from each other and secured the dogs' chains.

9

"Yours or rescue acquisitions?" His baseball cap shadowed his eyes, which gave them a sense of mystery.

"Mine." Something stirred in her stomach—the past. Thank God for the hat, as his eyes were beautiful to look into. And that's when she'd always found trouble. Trouble of the good kind.

The dogs barked wildly at the road, and a yellow lab ran through the yard.

"Who's let their precious dog run wild?" She approached the oncoming dog. "You're a friendly guy." She knelt. "Where did you come from?"

"He's a she, and her name is Blondie." Josef stepped beside Catherine.

"If you'll excuse me," Elaine said, "I'll let you two be. I'm ready for bed." Her aunt walked barefooted to the steps.

"I'll be in shortly, Aunt Elaine. It's been a long day, and I'm ready for bed, too."

"Don't hurry on my account, dear. You and Joe can catch up on things." At the top step, Elaine opened the door and sang sweetly, "Goodnight, Joe." It was obvious her aunt knew what she was doing by inviting Josef over this evening.

"Blondie—interesting name."

Josef crouched beside Catherine, and this time she connected with his brown eyes. Her heart pattered like a light rain on the barn roof. "Dagwood and Blondie, the comic strip. One of my favorites."

"Really? I don't think I knew that." She smiled for a second because she read the comic daily. "Well, you may want to keep her on a leash." At his deep-throated chuckle, she asked, "What?"

"Up here we don't lock up our animals. We train them. Blondie knows where she can and can't roam. She's fully aware of the road and, like a child, looks before crossing."

She strolled to the back of her pickup. "Well I—"

"Look, I know you're a vet and look out for animals, but she's safe. Trust me." His hand rested on top of hers. Warmth spread throughout her body, and she didn't like it. She didn't want to have this sort of reaction to Josef.

"I just don't want to be the one to tell you I told you so if anything happens to her." She lowered the tailgate of the truck.

"Elaine says you're staying for the weekend. Any plans?"

"I've scheduled someone to come look at the barn then I'm getting quotes for a conversion if it passes inspection."

"Conversion?" His face contorted in confusion.

"I can't put horses in a cow barn. The stalls will need to be reconfigured." She turned and faced him with her head cocked to the side, tipped down slightly with raised eyebrows, as if to say, *really*?

"How many horses do ya have?"

"Four right now. Do you know of anyone who'd like to buy one? Or two?" She yanked her duffle bag from the back and slung the strap over her shoulder before heading toward the house.

"Not off the top of my head, but I can put out the word for ya."

"I'd appreciate it. Well, I'd like to go and spend time with Elaine before she goes to bed."

"She's glad you're here. It's been too long, Cat. For both of us."

"Thanks, but you don't need to make me feel any guiltier than I already am. Wait! Us?"

"Elaine and me. I've missed you, too."

He stepped beside her, and she quickened her pace. His previous touch had her body reacting in ways she didn't want it to.

"Maybe we could go out tomorrow night for drinks. My treat." He matched her pace.

"We'll see."

Josef nodded, apparently deciding to leave the invitation like that rather than push her. "Come on, girl. Time to go." He patted his leg, and Blondie heeded his word, coming to stand beside him.

Josef sauntered across the lawn, and like a fool, she watched. He stood several inches taller than her five-seven. In ways, he looked like a farmer and in other ways, not. He carried weight like a farmer, but a healthy weight by her standards. He was clean—not covered in muck of sorts—and wearing a shirt and shorts. He glanced back as she assessed his legs and derriere. Instant heat flushed her face.

She stepped to the cement stairs leading to the house and touched the old wooden banister. Shivers coursed her body. Goose bumps covered her arms. She was back to being a youngster, sliding down the banister with a small bowl of ice cream in hand and jumping off in time, so as not to crash land. She used to sit on the step and stir the ice cream until it was the consistency of a malt. A great treat on a warm day. With a mental shake, she came back to reality.

The dogs looked at her. "Sorry, you'll be staying outside, guys." They lay down, and she felt a little better about leaving them out. "I'll bring you some water in a few minutes."

She opened the screen door to the welcoming smells of her past. Memories surrounded her. Fresh breads and pies baking lingered in her senses. She didn't realize how many memories there were tucked away for so long.

Ten years had passed since her last visit, and Catherine hadn't known what to expect. She stepped into the soft golden yellow kitchen, smaller than she remembered, and ahead to the right. In the corner sat the small metal Formica table and four chairs with their yellow marbled vinyl seat coverings. Uncle Gordon ate breakfast there every morning while the kids were at the big oak table.

From the kitchen, she walked into the large dining room with adjoining living room, both painted a light tan. Her hand slid over the dents and gouges the old oak dining room table had received through the years. Her aunt was in the bathroom so she went to the guest bedroom. Her room when she'd come stay for the summer. The old lavender and green floral wallpaper clung to the walls.

A new mattress and box spring sat in the white painted iron bed frame though. The old mattress had sagged so bad that if you shared the bed with anyone, you'd best like the person because you'd be getting very close under the covers in the middle.

She tossed the duffle bag into the seat of the old green armchair in the corner when her aunt stepped into the doorway.

"Hope you like the new bed. I know how much you'll miss the old one."

They both laughed, and Catherine's chest swelled with a loving warmth. She embraced her aunt. "The house looks good. Did you get new windows?"

"Yes, about five years ago. Trying to keep energy costs down, and it's working. I even had the company put up new siding. How about a cup of tea? I already have the water on. We can sit and talk."

"Sounds good." They walked to the kitchen. "Even the floors look good. They're better than the last time I was here."

"I had them resurfaced." Elaine sat at the small kitchen table. "It would've been a shame to let them go. The wood is so beautiful and even more so now that they've been redone."

"Who helps take care of the lawn? Don't tell me you do." Catherine went to the cupboard and took two floral teacups and matching saucers, carefully setting them on the counter.

"No, Joe takes care of it for me. He's the one who's maintained the barn and other buildings, too. But then again it's more of a benefit for him."

"What do you mean?" Catherine went to another cabinet and grabbed the tea tin, filling the tea ball before setting it in the ceramic teapot. Elaine cared only for loose-leaf tea, something Catherine had grown to appreciate.

"Well, he uses the barn for hay and also stores some of his farm equipment here."

"Oh." That explained the shiny green one in the shed. She'd have to get used to seeing him a lot if she moved to Oak City. She doubted she could handle that kind of drive every day. Catherine couldn't afford to hire someone or ask her aunt to care for the horses. Moving would more than likely be her only option if using the barn was a go.

"I'm sure you'll find the barn in fine shape so you can bring your horses here, and Joe is—"

The teakettle whistle pierced their conversation. Catherine removed the kettle and filled the serving pot.

As she carried the teapot and cups to the table, Elaine continued. "—more than willing to work with you. I'm sure he'd work out fair pricing on hay for the horses, too."

"Why does he have equipment stored here and not on his own property?"

"He leases the farming land from me."

"What do you mean leases it?"

"He pays me to farm my land. It's working out quite nicely. I paid for the work on the house with the money I made off Joe's farming.

Otherwise, I would've had to take out a loan. At my age that's not a good thing." Elaine poured tea into the cups. "Not only that, it's nice to see the land being farmed again rather than sitting empty with nothing growing but weeds. And I'm not about to sell it off either."

Catherine smiled. She hated to see Minnesota's farmland disappearing. It was vanishing at a fast rate. Urban growth had not been kind to the land.

"I'm glad to hear you're not selling because my horses need a home." Catherine sighed as she sipped her tea. This farm holds so many wonderful memories for me."

They each savored their tea, quiet for a moment, before Elaine spoke. "Joe's doing pretty good, Catherine. He hasn't married."

"Aunt Elaine," she scolded. "Stop trying to get us back together. I know you invited him over tonight."

"But you're moving back. Oh, you are planning on moving in with me, aren't you?" Her face lit with excitement as she took another sip.

"I'm waiting to see what becomes of the barn. But with your offer, I would love to have a temporary place to stay while I look for a permanent home. Not to mention a job." The teacup rolled back and forth in her hands.

"Oh, you should talk to Joe. Find out where he takes Blondie for vet care."

"If and when the time comes, I will." She stretched back in the chair, the long day catching up with her. "I'm exhausted from a busy day at work and the drive." Catherine set the cup on the matching saucer, and stretched her arms up and out over her head.

"What do you have planned for tomorrow?"

"I've arranged for a barn inspection then two different guys are coming to give me quotes on modifications to the barn. The stalls need to be adapted for horses." She finished the last of her chamomile tea.

"I never thought about changes. You would need to do that?"

"If this were temporary, I wouldn't. You know this isn't temporary, right?" She had never explained clearly to her aunt what she needed as far as the barn was concerned.

"Right." Elaine shook her head. "It's yours for as long as you need it."

"Then I need to look into making changes. Starting tomorrow." Catherine stood and took her teacup to the white porcelain sink. "Depending on how my day goes, I may take Josef up on his offer and go have a drink."

Chapter Three

By the end of the day, Catherine had the answers about the barn. It was a go. While getting ready to go out with Josef, Elaine knocked on her door.

"Catherine …" Elaine entered wearing her housecoat. "I want to give you something." She sat on the edge of the bed. "I want you to use this toward your rescue cause." She handed Catherine a folded check. "You and the animals need this."

"I—"

"Don't you refuse my donation. I want to do this, and now is the right time." Her aunt stood.

"Thank you. Thank you, Aunt Elaine." Tears welled up, and Catherine had a hard time speaking.

"Now stop that crying nonsense …" Her aunt gathered Catherine in her arms. "… or you'll have me crying as well. Plus, you don't want red, puffy eyes when Joe comes to pick you up for your date."

"It's not a date," Catherine huffed as she stepped from the embrace and swiped her cheeks dry. "We're going to the bar to have a few drinks." Her fingers pushed at the roots of her limp hair in hopes of adding a little volume.

"Well, I won't wait up for you. Just be ready to leave for church by eight-fifteen."

"I'll be ready." Catherine picked up the clock and set the alarm for seven-thirty, enough time to get dressed for church.

"Have a good night," her aunt crooned, exiting the room.

Catherine remembered the check in her hand and unfolded it. *Three thousand dollars?* She ran from the room shaking the piece of paper, yelling, "I can't take this, Aunt Elaine. This is too much."

"What did I tell you, child? Take the money, and don't deny me the satisfaction of helping your cause. Now finish getting ready because he's on his way."

Knowing she couldn't change her aunt's mind and aware that Josef was coming, Catherine trotted to her room and applied the remainder of minimal makeup she used. *Where the hell did she get the money?* Josef? Man, there's good money in land leasing, she guessed. Maybe this was money saved over time.

Coming around the corner into the kitchen, she found her aunt and Josef hugging. Elaine held an obvious fondness for Josef. More than she remembered.

"Are ya ready to go?" A gracious smile materialized over her aunt's shoulder.

"If you are."

Elaine and Josef let go of one another.

"This way then." His arm extended, gesturing to the back door. "Ladies first." He held the door open for her.

"Thanks." This wasn't a date, she reminded herself, as she stepped to the passenger side of his Chevy truck.

The interior of the truck surprised her. Spotless. Organized. Something she didn't expect for a guy and more so for a farmer. It should've been dirty and smelly.

"So where are you taking me?" she asked when he turned onto the gravel road. Brown eyes glanced her direction, and her stomach fluttered.

"The Watering Hole. It's probably not what you're used to, living in the cities, but the food could stand up to any one of those fancy-ass places."

"It'll be just fine. Notice I didn't dress up for the occasion." She gestured to her ensemble of shorts and layered tank tops. "I saved that for tomorrow morning."

"You're going to church?"

"Smart ass." She swung out and hit his thigh. A solid, muscular thigh. The flutter changed to a tingle. "You know Aunt Elaine. Die-hard

Catholic." They fell into their easy going, bantering relationship.

"That she is." They drove a short distance in silence before he asked, "So, what did ya find out about the barn?"

She turned sideways and couldn't help but grin. "Everything's set to go. The inspector mentioned using some of the wood already there to help save on cost, and one of the two renovators made the same comment. That made my decision easy because his price falls within my small budget.

"The contractor will take measurements and draw up plans for my approval. Once I approve the plans, he'll get the permits. It will be a few weeks, I'm sure, before anything gets started. As of right now, I'm not in any hurry to have things finished."

They turned onto the main road leading into town along the Snake River. Some boats had anglers, while others drifted on the water, taking leisurely evening rides.

"Why no hurry?"

"The place where the horses are boarded is still for sale. But I don't want to be caught off guard when the land sells, which could be in days, weeks … Well, you get the idea. My guess is sooner versus later."

"Why?"

"You sound just like a three year old." She whined, "Why? Why? Why?"

"Why?" His brown eyes held hers long enough to ignite the spark of the past deep within her soul.

"Knock it off." She delivered a light slap to his thigh. "The land is selling quickly in the area where the horses are located. Having Aunt Elaine's barn set up will help."

"How long have ya been at this rescue thing?"

"I'm in my second year with the horses. It started with cats and dogs. The horses struck me hard when I learned …" She averted her eyes and gazed out the window at the roadside. "Let's just say I didn't want to see a good animal put down because of one person's bad decision."

"How do you pay for their care and boarding? It's got to be expensive."

"It is. I've been lucky to receive donations of monetary value and merchandise. Feed, farrier, boarding all come in *way* under cost for me. I can't take in any more horses though, or it will break the bank."

They crossed over I-35 and entered Oak City.

"Wow, there's a Walmart now?"

"We may not be as civilized as you folks in the cities," Josef used a hillbilly accent, "but we do like to wear clothing and eat off of dishes."

"I didn't mean it like that," she giggled. "It's just that things have changed in the past ten years."

"As I said before, it's been too long since your last visit." Josef turned on Main Street.

Had she heard the tone in his voice correctly? Sorrow? Regret? Hope? Catherine glanced around. "Quite a few empty stores. Harvey's Hardware still in business? Is the old man still running it?"

"Yup, he puts in a few hours here and there."

She faced Josef with a smile. "Does he still have the five and dime candy?" Her smile broadened.

"Now look who's acting like a three-year-old."

"Sorry, but I love that stuff. You can't find it anywhere, or else I'm not looking in the right places."

"You'll have to stop in and say hi. Maybe pick up some. If I remember correctly, you liked Boston Baked Beans and those hard thin candies."

"Necco Wafers! You remember that?"

"There's a lot I remember about you."

There was the same tone again.

He pulled into a back parking lot. "We're here."

He hopped out of the truck and was by her side when she shut her door. With the back door labeled for deliveries, they strolled along the side of the building to the main entrance.

"That is so cool." Catherine stopped midway and took several steps into the parking lot. A mural covered the brick wall advertising the business name. "It looks like someone tagged the building."

"It was tagged on purpose. The cops found some kids tagging the rail cars. One of the kids belonged to the owner of the bar. The owner wasn't pleased. His daughter had to pay the fine." He slid his hand into hers, and they continued for the entrance. "He struck a deal with the kids and bought the supplies they needed. Gave them free rein on the project with some minor stipulations."

The Watering Hole was in one of the old brick business buildings. The front door was nestled in the middle, set back in an alcove. Neon alcohol advertisements brightened the three windows to each side of the door. Covered with shades, a person couldn't see through the windows.

"What happened to the kids after all of that?"

"I know the owner's daughter stayed out of trouble and is attending a school for the arts. One of the boys died while tagging. A train struck him. The other boy later committed suicide." He gripped the door handle. "Let's get a beer."

His hand slipped free from hers as he held the door open. She hadn't even noticed they held hands. It was as though her hand in his was a natural thing for them to do. Meant to be. A mental shake to clear her head and she stepped through into a dimly lit bar and restaurant. An old musty smell mixed with smoke from the years past hung in the air. She stood there waiting for her eyes to adjust and Josef to lead the way.

He took her hand again and weaved through crowded tables toward the back. "Do ya mind if we sit with my buddies? You remember Wayne, Elliott and Jackson?"

"Yeah, I remember them. They're still around, huh?"

No sooner said and they approached the table where the guys sat. They roared *Cat* and slid from the booth to give her hugs. Josef released her hand, and her heart ached at the loss.

"Man, you guys have grown. Good to see you." She welcomed the distraction.

"You, too. What brings you here?" Elliott released her from their embrace.

"Don't tell me you're here to see Joe?" Wayne pulled her in for his usual long hug.

"No! I'm visiting my aunt."

"Okay, my turn." Jackson placed his hand on Wayne's shoulder who stepped from the embrace. Jackson gave his big brother hug—a quick in and out delivery.

The booth accommodated five, so Josef let her slide in first then eased in next to her.

"Thanks." As she sat, she explained the purpose of being in town.

While having drinks and appetizers, they reminisced about the summer days she spent on her great-aunt and uncle's farm. "Do you guys remember that time we went fishing and I caught that enormous Sheepshead? You all had to take turns helping me reel that thing in." Cat smiled at the memory.

"Damned thing almost tipped the boat over," Wayne laughed.

"It wasn't the fish tipping the boat," Elliot interjected. "It was you and Joe leaning over the edge."

"Well, someone had to be there to get the damned fish into the boat." Josef took a swig of beer. "I remember how proud you were. You made us haul that stinky ass thing back to the farm, even after you found out the fish wasn't any good for eating."

"I'm still proud of catching that big thing." She swatted his bicep for teasing her. "But remember how Uncle Gordy didn't mind. He had us drag it to the back of the barn by the edge of the field and let the cats dig into it."

"Until the following morning when it stunk to high heaven." Josef plugged his nose, probably at the memory.

"Yeah." Catherine waved a hand in front of her face remembering. The rancid smell had blown through the open windows on a cool morning breeze, assaulted her nostrils and woke her. "I'm just glad it wasn't me who had to take the remains and bury them in the field."

The booth echoed with the roar of their laughter.

"We had some great bonfires, too. I remember a couple where you two," Elliot's finger waggled at her and Josef, "would disappear for a while."

Josef glanced her way. Her face warmed. "I remember *you* disappearing, too." She didn't want to talk about her past relations with Josef. "And not always with the same girl."

"Touché." Elliot held up his beer in acknowledgment of her comeback.

"Do any of you visit the old swimming hole?" Catherine's face warmed again, and she hoped it didn't show as a blush.

"No, they've built houses around it," Jackson stated, disappointed. "We sneak to the public beach late at night. Did you want to go for a swim?"

"Ah, no." She waved her hands. "No swimsuit."

"Who said we needed swimsuits." Wayne wiggled his eyebrows.

"You guys are just trying to get her naked and in trouble with the law." Josef looked at her, "They're only kidding. We don't go sneaking off at night. We leave that to the younger generation."

She listened as the guys recalled more stories over a couple more drinks. Taking a swig of beer, she glanced at her watch. Nearly eleven.

Catherine leaned into Josef's ear, "Do you mind if we go?"

"Hey, guys, we're taking off." Josef stood and threw some money on the table. "See ya after church."

"Good to see all of you. I'll see you around."

She and Josef walked to the truck, and he opened the door like a gentleman.

"Thanks," she said as Josef got in. "You still go to church, too, huh?"

"Every Sunday. The guys and I follow it up with lunch here at The Watering Hole." He fired up the truck and pulled out of the lot.

"Well, thanks for leaving the guys so early. It'll be hard enough for me to get up and get moving tomorrow. I like to sleep in and take it easy on Sunday mornings."

"So ya don't go to church?"

"Nope, it's been a while." She rested against the door, tipping her cheek onto the cool glass of the window.

"Well, as long as you're with your aunt, ya know she'll make ya go."

"I know. Something I'll have to get used to again."

The radio kicked out country tunes for the ride home. They pulled onto the dirt road leading to the farms.

"You don't need to take me back to Elaine's. I can walk across from your place."

"I don't mind."

"That's just stupid. Go back to your place."

"Wow, you're an easy girl."

"Only for animals."

"I can act like an animal." This earned him a slug to the shoulder. Her fist met a solid bicep. Damn, was he built.

"Ow, what was that for?" He rubbed his arm.

"Like you don't know. I'm talking four-legged-furry animals. Not party-sex-craved animals. So unless you're a werewolf, I won't take to you so easily."

"Werewolf, huh?" Josef parked the truck in his drive. "Can I walk ya home?"

"Sure." She gave into his request as she slid out, closed the door and met him behind the pickup. "It's so beautiful here. In the cities you don't get this kind of darkness, with the moon and stars lighting the night sky."

"It's even more beautiful having you back here."

"Jo … s … ef." Catherine stretched out his name in exasperation. But she couldn't look at him because something stirred in the depths of her heart. She wondered if he was trying to get back together with her. That ship had sailed and sunk at sea. Hadn't it?

Instead of pursuing the subject, Josef remained quiet as they walked.

They crossed the road and stepped onto grass. "I can make it the rest of the way. Thanks for a great night out. I needed it."

"You're welcome, and we'll see ya tomorrow."

Warm arms embraced her. More relaxed than normal after a few drinks, she didn't resist. Her head rested on his chest where his heart beat a slow rhythm. Strong. Steady. Relaxing. She exhaled then realizing what she was doing stepped from his arms.

"Tomorrow."

Chapter Four

The alarm sounded. Josef smacked the snooze button and rolled over. He tossed and turned to grab a few more winks, but it was no use. Cat was on his mind. The morning light peeked through the slats of the blinds.

After dropping her off, he'd had difficulty falling asleep. His feelings about his and Cat's past relationship were a jumbled mess. A mess like the pieces of a jigsaw puzzle dumped on a table, waiting to be put together. Could he still call it love? It was possible. He never had closure. She was the one to end it between them.

The whole purpose of growing closer, helping take care of Elaine and the farm, was his plan to '*win*' the farm from Elaine. Show her how much the land meant to him by giving the farm life again. Elaine held a fondness for him. Josef hoped she'd remember him when it mattered most.

He wanted the farmland's fertile soil that produced crops. He wanted the farmland that brought him a profit. He wanted the farmland that once belonged to his great granddaddy.

But with Cat back in the picture and possibly living with Elaine, and Elaine knowing about Cat's rescue mission, Cat could take it all away from him. Yup, Cat was going to give him a run for his money.

His dreams that night had been filled with her and the memories of their past. Sneaking into the darkness of night to the barn, spreading out the hidden blanket and exploring each other's bodies and needs.

"Damn woman." He threw the covers back. "She left me once. And now she's back in my life." He turned the alarm off as the phone rang.

"Hello."

"Josef, I need you to come over. Aunt Elaine is gone."

He sat in his boxers on the edge of the bed at the sound of her distraught voice.

"What do ya mean, gone?"

Her voice, shaky and filled with tears, stated, "Dead."

"I'm on my way." He slid into last night's jeans and pulled a clean shirt from his dresser. Not bothering with socks or shoes, he ran down the hall and through the front door for Elaine's.

Stones stabbed his feet as he darted across the gravel road. The pain in his feet didn't compare to the pain in his heart. He raced through the grass to where she sat on the back step. "Cat, I'm here." He knelt with open arms, and she fell into them sobbing.

"I didn't ... hear her up ... and went to ... her room."

"Okay. Have ya called anyone else?" He needed to remain calm for her.

"No," she wailed with grief. "I didn't know who to call. You were the first one I thought of."

"Okay. I'll be right back." To make sure of the situation, he went inside to check on Elaine.

In her room, Elaine rested on the bed and appeared at peace. By her side, he placed two fingers at her throat for a pulse. Nothing. His throat constricted, he swallowed and wiped the tears from his cheek. "Rest in peace, Elaine. May God be with you." Bowing his head, a few more tears fell.

Swiping his eyes, he'd stay strong for Cat. She would need him with no family around. Stepping outside, his stomach clenched at the site of Cat hunched over on the step. "Let's get your things and go back to my place."

"I don't—"

"If ya don't want to leave ya don't have to. I—I just thought you'd be more comfortable over at my house."

"Yeah, okay." She stood and inched through the yard, not going back inside to pack or get the dogs.

His hand rested on the small of her back, and they made their way across the forty plus yards to his farm. They could get her things later.

She sat on the closest chair in the living room.

"I'll be right back." He went to the kitchen and returned with a box of tissue. "We need to make some calls, Cat." He knelt by her side and touched her arm. "Are ya up to that?"

Her head shook as if haunted by inner pain. Her legs were pulled up, arms wrapped around, to hold and hug herself. Eyes transfixed on her toes.

"Okay. I'm going to call the police and then your mom." A faint pat on her arm and he stood. "I'll be outside if you need me." In the kitchen, he turned on the coffee pot, took a bottle of water from the fridge and returned to the living room. He set the water bottle on the round table and went outside to make the call.

"Oak City police. My name is Barbara. How can I assist you?"

"Hi, Barbara, Josef Garrison."

"Hey, Josef. What can I do for you?" Barbara being a high school classmate and friend didn't make the situation any easier for him.

"Elaine Jenkins passed away. Her great niece, Catherine Mornelli, is here visiting. This morning Cat woke to find Elaine ... dead."

"Oh, poor thing. I'll send someone out right away. Can you give me the address?"

Josef gave the details and hung up. He dialed Cat's mom's number and while waiting for Margaret to answer, Blondie sat in front of him. "Sorry girl, you'll have to wait until I make these calls. I'm guessing we'll need to take care of Darby and Fuzzy, too."

The phone continued to ring, but he hung up when the call went to voice mail. You didn't leave a message like this on voice mail. He went back inside and stopped beside the chair where Cat sat, placed a hand on her shoulder and asked, "Do your parents go to church?" With her nod, he left to sit on the front porch.

If her parents were at church, they wouldn't have their cell phones on and with no phone numbers for other family members, he stared across to the Jenkins farm. He pressed Margaret's name, and the phone rang. When the voice mail kicked on he waited for the infamous tone. "Hi Margaret, this is Josef. It's Sunday, June tenth, and it's nearing ten o'clock. If you could please call me when you get this, I'd appreciate it. Thanks."

Josef entered the house. "Let's sit on the couch."

Cat stood and joined him where he sat. She leaned into his chest, and he folded his arm around her.

"I couldn't get a hold of your parents. I left a simple message for them to call me. And the police are on their way. They'll more than likely need to talk to ya. Okay?"

"Okay," her voice cracked as she dissolved into tears.

"I need to feed Blondie, and I'm guessing you haven't fed Fuzzy and Darby."

"Oh, no." Cat sat straight. "I forgot about them."

"Don't worry. I'll take care of them. Where's their food?"

"Inside the door on the floor. You'll see it." Wounded eyes gazed at him, and his throat tightened. "Thank you," she whimpered through swollen lips.

"I'll be back." Outside, Josef fed Blondie. A car kicked up dust heading in his direction. He went inside. "The cops are coming. If they need to speak to ya, I'll bring them here." Not looking for a response from her, he left and crossed to Elaine's. Oak City's finest pulled into the drive as he crossed the road.

"Hey, Joe." The officer exited his squad car. "I hear Mrs. Jenkins passed away."

"Dale." Josef reached to shake his friend's hand. "Yeah, Cat found her this morning."

"Where's Cat?" Dale strolled across the front lawn.

"Over at my place." He trailed Dale. "This morning Cat went to check on Elaine, and well, you know."

"Okay, thanks." Dale entered the house, and Josef followed. "You don't need to come with me."

"I'm not. I need to feed Cat's dogs, and the food is somewhere in here." He gestured around the kitchen. "Here it is. I'll be outside." Josef grabbed the bucket and stepped outside.

Dog bowls filled, he sat on the swing hanging from the big oak tree. Sadness filled his heart at the loss of Elaine. As much as he wanted the land, he never wished death upon her. She was a sweet, dear old family friend. She was a grandmother figure to him. She was Cat's great-aunt.

"Yeah, she's passed on. Probably had a heart attack in her sleep."

27

Dale let the screen door slam closed. Josef turned to face him. "You'll want to contact the funeral home. With no crime committed here, we don't need to be involved."

"Okay. I'm waiting to hear from Cat's parents. They're the only family I know how to reach. Cat's mom will know who to call."

"Well, I'm done here." Dale and Josef sauntered to the squad car. "You playing poker this week?"

"Hell, yeah. I wouldn't miss a night."

"Well, give my condolences to Cat, and we'll see you Wednesday night."

"Will do." Josef delivered a firm slap to Dale's shoulder blade before the officer maneuvered into the car. "Stay safe, man."

"Always." Dale closed the door.

Josef waited for Dale to leave before crossing the road home. His cell phone rang, and he sat on the first piece of solid furniture he could find. "Hi, Margaret."

"Josef, what's wrong? Is Catherine alright?"

"Catherine's fine."

Apprehensive, Margaret asked, "Is it Elaine?"

"Yes." He gave her a moment before speaking. "Cat awoke this morning and found Elaine still in bed. The police said to call the funeral home, and they'll take care of her. I have no knowledge of Elaine's wishes and don't know how to reach other family members. Can you handle things?"

"Yes," Margaret whispered through the phone line.

"I'll help in any way I can."

"Could you call the funeral home for me?" Margaret sniffled. "I don't want her to remain in the house longer than necessary. Did they say how she died?"

"I'll make the call. The officer presumed a heart attack since she was sleeping. Nothing looked suspicious."

"Okay, thanks." She paused. "Where's Catherine?"

"She's here with me. Would you like to speak to her?"

"Please."

"Just a minute." Josef walked through the front door and in a few strides stood by the couch. "I was outside. Here she is." He handed the cell to Cat and whispered, "It's your mom."

"Hi Mom … I'm fine. Josef's been great." She left the couch and shuffled to the back patio.

He didn't follow. This was a private conversation. Her eyes were swollen, red and moist from crying. He'd leave her alone to take care of things. Something he didn't want to do but had to.

She came inside and handed the phone to him. "She needs to talk to you."

"Margaret? Let me get some paper." He hurried to the kitchen. "Okay, give me the info." He scribbled the name and number of the funeral home. "I'll call them now. What are your plans?"

"I'm leaving as soon as I'm packed and have called the rest of the family. Elaine has a sister who lives close by and will probably arrive before I get there." She paused. "Cat's leaving and coming home. Make sure she's okay to drive. Okay, Josef?"

"I will." He struggled to find the right words to say. "I'm sorry. I really cared for Elaine. She'll be missed."

"Thank you, Josef. I'll see you soon."

He slid the phone into his jeans pocket, then joined Cat in the living room, but she was gone. He hadn't heard her leave. Through the screen door he scanned both yards. A door slammed. She'd returned to Elaine's. Back in the kitchen, he poured a cup of coffee and called the funeral home. He'd see Cat before she left.

Chapter Five

Catherine stepped into the kitchen. Quiet. Still. Heaviness filled her chest. She couldn't breathe. The brightly lit yellow kitchen faded to grey, and she caught the counter. Holding on for support. Holding on to the memories.

At a turtle's pace, she observed every minuscule detail of what had been a part of her life on the farm. Gone now. Gone forever. What would become of the farm? What were her great-aunt's plans? What was *she* going to do? She was set to move the horses and maybe herself. *Now what?*

One foot stepped in front of the other. A natural motion for the body to do yet she struggled to shuffle through the kitchen and into the dining room, then into the hall between the two bedrooms. To the left her aunt lay in a peaceful slumber. The floodgate opened. Catherine's head jerked right, and her body followed as she dashed into her room. She flung herself on the bed, landing on her stomach, and curled into the fetal position.

"There, there, child." Aunt Elaine's voice. But how?

Catherine squeezed her eyes. She didn't want to look. This was crazy. She was hearing things.

"I'm at peace with God."

"Aunt Elaine?" Her eyes remained closed.

"Yes, child, I am with you, but I need to go."

"No. Stay with me."

"It will all work out."

"I love you," she blubbered, stuffing her face into the mattress.

"Cat?" A man's voice echoed through the empty house.

"Josef?" She lifted her head enough to peer through sore wet eyes. "Josef, she was here—speaking to me—just now."

"It's okay. I'm here." He sat on the bed, and she lifted her head onto his thigh. He stroked her hair while soothing, "It'll be okay."

"What do I do now? I was going to bring the horses here, and now she's gone."

"You'll figure it out, Cat. You always do. Who knows … maybe she has a will, and she'll leave the farm to ya."

"I doubt that. Plus, you were closer to her in the end than I was. I stayed away for too long." She sobbed. "I should've visited. I should've made the time to come back, but I didn't and now—" He continued to comfort her while she rode the roller coaster of emotions. Saddened by the loss, yet angry at herself. "Now she's gone. I won't ever see her again."

She sat wiping her eyes and nose with a tissue. "I need to pack and go home." Up now, she haphazardly threw items in the duffle bag. "I need to sort things out. Make some calls." She wept all the way to the bathroom to gather her items. "Take care of my mom, Josef. As far as I know, my dad is staying in the cities until the funeral."

"Are you coming back for the funeral?"

"Of course."

He filled the doorframe, and those brown eyes—those damned eyes—expressed concern and warmed her heart.

This wasn't the time or place for her to have these feelings. She wanted to go into his arms. To be loved. To be comforted. To be told it would be okay.

"Excuse me." She dipped under his arm and entered the bedroom.

"Ya sure you're okay to drive? I don't want anything to happen to ya."

"I'm okay. I'll be fine."

His head tipped to the side, his thick eyebrows scrunched together, and his mouth quirked.

"I promise. I'm fine. Don't worry about me." She grabbed the duffle bag and her keys. Glancing around the old room one last time, she swallowed the lump in her throat and hustled outside.

"I can worry if I want. Plus, I promised your mom I'd make sure you were okay before ya left."

"If I have difficulties driving," she tossed the bag in the back end of her truck, "I promise I'll pull over to the side of the road. Okay?" She went inside, got the dogs' food container and tossed it inside the pickup.

"Okay."

"I really can't—" She unleashed the dogs from the chains and pulled the stakes from the yard. "Do your business, boys. We're going for a ride." As the dogs scurried around, she continued talking with Josef, "I can't say thanks enough for what you've done for me this morning. I don't know what I would've done without you." She held the back door of the truck open for the dogs to jump in the back seat.

"Cat—"

"I really appreciate it." Catherine embraced him and pecked his cheek before hopping into the cab of the truck. "I'll see you at the funeral."

She pulled slowly out of the driveway, onto the road and waved to him through the open window. There was the situation with the horses—where would she board them?

Then her mind turned to the man she'd left standing alone. Staying at the farm or Josef's would've been a mistake. She couldn't trust herself right now around him. She needed to get home. Away from him.

* * * *

Catherine followed her parents into the lawyer's small wood paneled office. She had received the call from her mother. Seemed there might be a glimmer of hope. Maybe Josef's crazy hair-brained idea wasn't so crazy after all. Maybe she would get the farm.

Familiar faces filled the small quiet room. Elaine's remaining siblings, a sister and a brother, sat whispering to each other at the long oak table. Two faces didn't belong to the family, and she wondered why Josef and a priest were in attendance.

Margaret made introductions. "Catherine, this is Mr. Griffon, Elaine's attorney."

"Nice to meet you." Catherine shook the tall, thin man's narrow hand.

"Nice to meet you as well, though I regret the occasion for our meeting. Please have a seat, and we'll get started." Mr. Griffon gestured to some empty chairs.

Catherine struggled to focus on the attorney and the will proceedings. Distractions came too easy. Josef sat clean-cut and shaven in a business suit. God, he looked good. But what was he doing there?

At the mention of her name, her ears perked like a mouse hearing the approach of a cat on the prowl.

"… to receive the two hundred acres of farming land."

"What?"

Mr. Griffon stopped at Catherine's outburst. She covered her mouth when she saw the disapproving glances.

The lawyer continued reading. "If at the time of my death and the reading of my last will and testament Josef Gustav Garrison, residing at Rural Route ten, Oak City, Minnesota, 55987, is under contract to lease the two hundred acres, the contract remains binding until the end of its term."

Great, she not only inherited the land, but the contract with Josef.

"I, Elaine Elizabeth Jenkins, leave the house and farm buildings and the twenty acres upon which they reside to Josef Gustav Garrison…"

Catherine twisted a section of hair and tuned out the lawyer for a moment. Had her great-aunt lost her mind? She screwed it up. Catherine should've gotten the buildings, and Josef should've gotten the land. Now what was she going to do? She shredded the check her great-aunt gave her after a long mental battle of whether to cash or not cash? She struggled with taking money she no longer felt was hers to take.

The legal jargon of what the brother and sister would receive, which didn't sound like much, garbled in her ears. She stared at Josef, twisting her hair tighter and tighter. The exchange of disbelieving gazes between their eyes was mutual.

"… Mornelli marries within ninety days of the reading of my will, a Trust Fund will take effect the day of the marriage, wherein she will receive twenty-five thousand dollars over the course of the first five years of her marriage, at the rate of five thousand dollars per year."

"What the hell?" Catherine exclaimed, slapping her hands on the table. *That* got her attention! Had Aunt Elaine gone totally nuts?

Mr. Griffon shot her a stern look indicating he'd brook no more such outbursts.

Her finger located a section of hair and twisted, re-looping the hair around and around and around.

Mr. Griffon continued with the reading. "If Catherine Elaine Mornelli and her spouse celebrate their sixth year wedding anniversary date, she will receive an additional sixteen thousand dollars. If Catherine Elaine Mornelli and her spouse have children, for every child born, up to four children, I, Elaine Elizabeth Jenkins, leave five thousand dollars for each child in a college savings fund."

The difficult need to remain quiet drove her fidgeting to the highest state. Feet crossed and uncrossed. Knees wiggled and bounced. Finger twisted and untwisted hair. Ears rang, unable to believe what she'd heard.

Words continued to flow out of the attorney's mouth, but they went unheard. Questions and thoughts bounced in her head like a rubber ball. Her stomach couldn't take much more as it backed up into her esophagus.

The room dissolved around her as she stared into nothingness. How could her aunt ask her to do this? How could she put such stipulations on Catherine's inheritance?

She couldn't move or speak. She looked around the table. The reading had concluded. The priest from the church, her mother, Josef and Elaine's siblings tossed questions at Mr. Griffon. The man was up against a firing squad.

She stood. "I don't feel well," she choked out and bolted from the room.

In the closet-sized women's restroom, Catherine sat on the closed toilet seat. It hadn't been an excuse—the stomach bile maneuvered further up her throat. The thought of the farm and marriage—*marriage*—was overwhelming.

"Catherine, are you all right?"

"I'm fine, Mom. I just need a moment, please."

"Okay. We'll be waiting for you outside in the parking lot."

Catherine took a deep breath and counted to ten before stepping from the bathroom. A few more deep breaths and she slipped on her sunglasses. Strolling through the door onto the sidewalk, she sucked warm fresh air into her lungs, replacing the musty dry air of the attorney's office. She turned the corner of the building to see her mother in a conversation with Josef. She backed around the corner and sat on a wooden bench against the brick wall.

At last, she stood and approached the gold Buick.

"Goodbye, Josef." Margaret embraced him. "We'll talk to you soon."

Without a word to Catherine he strolled away.

"Are you feeling well enough to have lunch?" Her mother asked, standing between their car and her pickup.

"That would be fine." Maybe food would help. "I'll follow you."

In disbelief, the questions continued to run amuck through her head. Why was marriage part of all of this?

A short ride to the restaurant and the hostess seated Catherine and her parents in a booth. After the woman left the table, her mother brought up the will. "Catherine, if you marry, the trust fund will help you and the animals."

"Marry?" Catherine squeaked then softened her tone. "In ninety days?"

"It's possible." Her mother picked up a menu to peruse.

Was she insane? Was marriage even possible? *Who would I marry?*

"No, I don't think marriage is possible, Mom. What about the animals? Where would I move with them? Whoever I marry would have to love animals and stand beside me through this?"

"What about Josef?"

"Josef? What do you mean *Josef?*" Her voice hitched then settled into a quiet mumble. "Josef? Would Josef be willing? We did have a connection—once. No. Been there, done that. It didn't work out for us."

Her mother set down the menu. "Well, neither of you are married, and I just thought with your history—well, I just thought." She picked up the menu again.

"Why was the priest there?"

Her father kept his eyes on the menu and his mouth shut until the five-foot-four round waitress approached.

"My name is Stephanie, and I'll be your server. Are you ready to order?" she asked with a smile. Her brown hair was contained in a bun at the nape of her neck.

"I'm ready. How about you ladies?" Her father looked to Catherine and her mother and with their nods ordered first.

When Stephanie ambled away with their orders, her mother continued, "Didn't you hear what the attorney said?"

"When he mentioned *marriage* and *trust fund*, I sort of zoned out." Stephanie's interruption had given her a moment to regain control of her emotions.

"Well, if you marry and divorce within five years, the trust fund comes to an immediate end. You lose *all* remaining funds to the Catholic Church. That's why Father Tim was at the reading of Elaine's will."

"And if I don't marry?" A section of hair twisted through her fingers.

"If you decide not to marry, you only have the land. And Josef continues to farm the land until his lease agreement ends."

"I can't believe she had the audacity to put marriage—and children too—into her will." This took the cake. Her great aunt had thought of everything. "Why, Mom?"

"You meant a lot to Elaine, and she was a very savvy woman when it came to business. Just take it, and don't question why."

"It's not a matter of *taking*, Mother. It's a matter of whether or not I choose to marry. Not only that, I have to find someone who'll marry me in ninety days. Did I miss anything else while in my state of shock?"

Catherine noticed Stephanie's diamond ring as she set their plates on the table. "How long have you been married?"

"Oh, I'm not married yet. This is an engagement ring." She blushed. "We're getting married in a year."

"Congratulations," they all said in unison.

"Thank you. I'll be back to check on things." Stephanie strolled away.

"You didn't miss anything else." Her mom stirred her soup.

Catherine poured dressing over her salad. "So what it comes down to is either I get married and get the money, or I don't get married and get stuck with land I can't use for two years?" She mixed the dressing into her salad.

"Yes." Her mother took a bite of her sandwich, chewed and swallowed. "Josef has done very well for himself, Catherine. You might want to pay him a visit."

Overwhelmed by all she had heard, there was plenty to contemplate. She had three months to decide whether to get married or not. Did the money make it worth her while to marry someone? And who was she going to find to marry her in a short time frame? Josef?

Chapter Six

Josef sat in his pickup when Catherine and her parents left the parking lot of the attorney's office, headed north on Main Street. He turned the key, and the Chevy Silverado came to life, vibrating his seat. He grabbed his shades off the dash and slid them onto his face. Before long, the June sun would retreat into the land bringing relief from the humid air.

On Main Street, he turned left to go home, and the sun glared through the windshield. The future could hold promise. He smiled. Land and a wife. But … would Cat marry him? Would the money be a deal maker or breaker? If he wanted the family land back, he'd do whatever it took. The money didn't matter to him—all he wanted was the land. The land his great-granddaddy lost in a poker bet to Cat's great granddaddy.

He crossed over Highway I-35 and followed the winding road along the Snake River before turning toward home. The memories of when he was a teenager came back. Discovering girls. Looking forward to Cat's visits to Elaine and Gordon's for the summer months. The summer before her senior year, they began dating. She was sixteen, and he was eighteen.

They had attended a wedding, and at the reception, he asked her to dance to a slow song. When the music ended, she took him by the hand and led him outside. They exchanged their second kiss. Their first kiss was in the hayloft when he was eight and Cat was six. But the second kiss led to a summer of learning and growing. Cat wouldn't have sexual intercourse with him, but oral sex was another story.

He turned onto the gravel road and shook his head. With heated thoughts of Cat, he needed a cool shower. As he approached the drive, he stopped, turning his glance to where Elaine's house sat empty. He would do whatever he could to get the land back into his family's hands.

He pulled his cell phone from the inner suit pocket and selected the number. "Margaret, it's Josef. Can I speak to Cat?"

He heard the phone's muffled static.

"What do you need, Josef?" Cat answered without a greeting. "The contract is binding. You have your land. I have nothing." He heard the bitterness in each word as she spoke them.

"Cat, I'm sorry. Can we talk? Can ya come to the house before ya leave?"

"What could we possibly have to talk about that you can't talk about over the phone?" Anger came through the line this time.

"Please come. I'd rather talk to ya in person. Alone." Out of the truck, he went inside.

"Fine." She surrendered to his plea. "I'll be there in about thirty minutes."

"Okay." He set the phone on the kitchen island as Blondie came to his side. "Need to go out, girl?" Her tail wagged, earning a pat on the head. "Can't get my good suit covered in fur. Out ya go," and he held the back door to the garage open for her.

The tone of the phone conversation cooled the need for a shower, and his suit hung in the back of the closet again. Lucky for him the thing still fit. He never thought about trying the suit on prior to the will reading. Stripped down to nothing but his skivvies, he decided after sitting in a stuffy office and a suit, a quick rinse would feel good after all.

Refreshed, he pulled on a tee shirt and shorts. Gravel crunched, and Blondie barked excitedly. A vehicle door closed. He sat on the stairs out of sight and listened.

"Hey, Blondie. How you doing, girl? Where's Josef?" Cat received several low barks from the dog.

She knocked on the door and yelled his name.

He turned the corner. "Come on in. Can I get you something to drink?"

"I'm fine, thanks." They walked into the living room. "What's so important that we need to talk right now? In person." She sat in a chair.

"I wanted to know about your plans." He sat in the matching chair, separated by a round table. "Ya know, with the will and all?"

"Jesus, Josef." She turned, piercing him with her eyes as her voice turned fierce. "I don't know. We only found out, what? Two, three hours ago, and you want to know what I'm planning on doing?"

"I'm asking because of your horses." She looked away from him. "Neither of us got what we wanted. I doubt ya have funds to build on the land, and if ya did, you can't build until my contract ends. Unless I break the lease."

Her head whipped around to face him. "Would you do that for me?" she asked excited and anxious. "Would you break the lease agreement?"

He remained silent. "No, I won't break the contract. I'm sorry. I didn't mean to—"

"Then why the hell did you even bring it up?" Her arms flailed about as she rose, and he stood, too.

"Please sit down." He paused, and when she didn't sit he asked again.

Defiant with arms across her chest, she returned to the chair.

"Thank you." He sat beside her. "I'm trying to understand your thoughts."

"What thoughts? I haven't a clue as to what I'm going to do. I know I'm going to continue to take your money for the land you're farming." The hint of a smirk was better than her scowling and angry.

"Cat, would you want to work out an agreement for use of the barn with my land contract? You could still make the necessary changes needed to the barn for the horses."

"So I'd have a barn for the horses," she stated irritated, "but where am I going to stay? I don't—"

"I didn't think about that. Of course Elaine's house would be empty, but that would be entirely up to you."

"It's something to think about. Thank you." She softened up some.

They sat a moment in silence before Josef spoke. "That marriage trust fund was interesting. What did ya make of that?"

"It's insanity. I'd love to know what my aunt was thinking when she wrote that part." She paused quickly to add, "And all that money. Where did she get it?"

"You've got me. But she wasn't insane. Elaine was one hell of a woman." He decided to go on a fishing expedition, prepared for her emotional tilter whirl. "So, are you going to tell your boyfriend that if he marries ya you get a large sum of money?"

"I don't have one, and if I did, I don't know as if I'd say anything. Happy?" she huffed.

"About what?" he asked, befuddled by her question.

"That I don't have a boyfriend. The trust fund is out of reach. The church will end up with it."

"What if someone were to ask you to marry them?" he blurted, as he waited with moist palms and a fluttering stomach.

"Are you asking, Josef?"

"If I was, what would ya say?" His heart raced rampant like Blondie chasing a rabbit. There was the possibility of her saying yes and him getting the land back in the family name.

"Why? Are *you* asking?"

"Maybe." He swallowed hard. Was he really doing this? Asking her to marry him?

"Maybe? Jesus, Josef." Cat stood and walked to the door. "I can't talk about this anymore. I need to get home."

Disappointed but not sure why, he joined her in the foyer. "I'll talk to ya soon, Cat. Drive carefully." Once she was out of the house, he wiped his palms on his pant legs and jumped up and down, in hopes of getting the flutters out of his stomach.

With a marriage to Cat, they would each get what they wanted. He would get the land back into the rightful hands of his family, and she would have a place and money for her rescue operation.

How serious was he about marriage? It was a thought. The words had escaped before he thought out the situation. He needed to let it mull around in both of their heads before taking any further actions.

* * * *

Josef attended late Mass on Sunday morning and waited in line to say good morning to Father Tim. He shook the middle-aged man's hand. "Great sermon today, Father."

"Thank you, Josef." Father released their hands. "Elaine's trust monies will be a very welcomed gift to our church community."

"Oh, have you spoken to Catherine?" To hear Father speak of the fund shocked him.

"No, but I don't believe she's engaged."

"Well, I think we need to wait and see what happens. The Lord works in mysterious ways. Right, Father?"

"He does indeed, Josef. He does indeed."

"Have a good day." He left Father standing on the stairs with a bewildered look.

A firm hand slapped him on the shoulder.

"Are we meetin' at The Watering Hole?" his best friend Wayne asked.

"Yeah, I need to talk to someone." He stepped off the last step of the church and onto the sidewalk.

"Your brothers aren't around to talk to?" Wayne's six foot, two-hundred and forty-pound body maneuvered the church crowd well.

"No, not when I need to talk to someone right now. Nice friend you are."

"You know I'm kiddin'. Anything to do with the Jenkin's will?"

Josef turned to see who was in earshot. "You could say that. I'll see you there." Ten minutes later, he pulled into the parking lot of The Watering Hole.

Located in the back corner, by the kitchen and band stage, he slid onto the well-worn wooden seat of the booth they sat at every Sunday. No fancy napkins, only paper at The Hole. A hard plastic glass held the mismatched silverware.

"Hey, Joe. The usual?" Bridget asked from the bar.

He nodded at the twenty-two year old, electric blue-eyed, curvaceous, blonde college waitress. He loved the constant flirting between them, but it stopped there. She was too young for him.

Wayne strolled in with Elliot and yelled, "Make it three, Bridget."

"Already on it." The beer flowed from the tap nozzle into mugs.

"I hear you need to talk to us." Elliot slid on the bench. Elliot was smaller than Wayne and Josef. They became best friends in the fifth grade when Elliot's family moved into town.

"Wait till Bridget gets here with our drinks."

As if on cue, she approached with three beers and a basket of chips and The Hole's homemade salsa.

"Thanks, Bridget," all three said in unison.

Josef took a swig of beer with Wayne and Elliot before stating, "Elaine didn't leave me the farm."

"What? Why not?" they exclaimed.

"I got the twenty acres the farm house and buildings sit on, while Cat got the two hundred farming acres. To top it off, Elaine left Cat a trust fund with one stipulation—she has to get married."

"Why does she have to get married for the money?" Elliot asked, glancing from Josef to Wayne and back again.

"I'm not sure. Anyways, the only way I'm going to get that land back is to marry Cat."

The two men nearly choked on their nachos and quickly took gulps of their beers.

"You're getting married?" Wayne asked, shocked.

"I somewhat already asked her."

"And what did she say?" Elliot asked, shoving a chip loaded with salsa into his mouth.

"I approached it more as a question of "what if". If she doesn't get married, the church gets the trust fund."

"Oh," Wayne stated, "that's why you didn't say anything after Mass."

"Does she have a boyfriend?" Elliot received Wayne's elbow at his question. "What? There might already be someone in the picture."

"No boyfriend. Asked her before I brought up the question of marriage."

"When are you going to propose the right way?" Wayne took another gulp of beer.

"Not sure, but I'll be talking to her."

* * * *

Two weeks had passed since they last talked. Josef paced from the living room into the front hall while the phone rang. Two weeks since he asked Cat about marriage. Marriage to him.

"Hello?" came breathless through the line.

"Cat, Josef. This a good time?" He walked around the kitchen and through the hall in the dining room.

"Yeah, I was outside with the dogs. What's up?"

"What do ya have planned for the week of the Fourth of July?" While working in the fields, Cat and marriage had filled his thoughts the past two weeks. Time to take action before time ran out for her.

"Nothing much. Why?"

"I was hoping ya could take time off and come visit. You can stay at my place." He wanted to propose in person.

"What purpose do I have for coming up there? And I'm not staying with you," she stated flatly.

"I'd like to talk. In person." He was back in the living room, staring out the big open patio windows.

"Josef, we've already talked. There's no reason for me to come there." She spoke with a defensive tone.

"Is it possible? For you to come?" He remained calm despite her irritation.

"I don't know."

"Please?" Whining was beneath him, but at the moment, it was the only way. "If not the week, then at least the weekend? You could stay at Elaine's." Silence. "Cat, please."

"Plan on the weekend, and … I would very much like to stay at the old farm house. I won't be there until Saturday morning though."

"Thank you. My parents have a great Fourth of July family gathering, and I was hoping we could go together."

"If I can take the time off, that would be nice. I'll see you Saturday."

Her line went dead.

He had a week to find the right diamond. He had a week to find the right setting. He had a week to find the right words.

Chapter Seven

Catherine parked in Elaine's drive and scanned the expansive gap to Josef's place. Although over three weeks had gone by, did she make a mistake in returning to the farm so soon after her aunt's passing? Did she make a mistake taking the week off? She had a good idea about what he wanted to talk about—marriage.

"Okay, boys, let's get those leashes on and get you tethered. Fritz, I'll help you down." No one had come forward for the injured dog. Darby and Fuzzy welcomed him into the house with joy and enthusiasm. The cats not so much.

She paused at the bottom step leading to the house. Staying could be a challenge with fresh memories. Her heart accelerated, and sweat beaded on her forehead, neck and chest. If she couldn't stay at Elaine's, she'd have to stay with Josef.

A calmness settled on her as a teasing breeze swept her shoulders. She wanted to be here. The house was open, and cool wind rushed past when she stepped through the door. She strolled through the kitchen, entered the dining room and found the windows and front door open. *Josef.*

As she went outside, the dogs barked, and Blondie darted across the lawn. The dog stopped for a moment of acknowledgement from Catherine before bounding to Darby and Fuzzy. She then paused to sniff Fritz. With her nose's approval, Blondie invited Fritz to play by the old oak tree.

Of course Blondie's owner wasn't far behind. "I opened up the windows to get fresh air moving around."

"Thank you. I appreciate it." She opened the tailgate of the truck. "I need to get unloaded and settled."

"Can I help with anything?" His hand rested on hers on the tailgate.

"I'll be fine. Thanks. You've done enough."

"Who's the big dog?" He pointed toward the dogs.

"That's Fritz. He was rushed in for emergency surgery after being struck by a car and then a truck." She pulled the duffle bag forward, swung it onto her shoulder and grabbed a box. "No one claimed him, so he's with me until I find him a home. A home with a lot of running space."

"A farm would be a good home." He followed her toward the house.

"You know of someone?"

"I'll let ya know if someone comes to mind. Listen, can ya come for dinner this evening. We can talk then. Say six o'clock?" He held the door open for her.

"Sounds good." Catherine stepped inside.

"I'll see ya then." He closed the door and at the bottom step said, "Let's go, Blondie." He patted his leg, and the dog bounded to his side. She never tired of his rear view.

Inside everything was gone. There wasn't a stick of furniture in the house. Aunt Elaine's siblings didn't waste time removing their share of belongings. Her mother mentioned an estate sale to clear out the unwanted items.

She had some cleaning to do before going to Josef's. Finding the dogs' food and water bowls in the box, she set them on the counter next to the radio and hit the play button. Carrie Underwood's latest CD belted from the speakers. Rag in one hand and cleaning solution in another, she got to work.

Once the bathroom was clean she attacked the kitchen then opened the refrigerator, which she considered an antique, and wiped the shelves. She emptied the cooler, packed with refrigerated items for her stay. With time to spare, she set the inflatable mattress up in the living room, showered and changed for dinner.

* * * *

Beautiful as a teenager, Cat got better with age. Shorts gave way to her long legs and round bottom, and the snug fitting tee shirt hugged the curves up top. No longer thin as a rail, her fat and muscles were proportioned in all the right places. She was perfect for him.

He had frozen store-bought lasagna, garlic bread from the bakery, frozen corn off the cob from his own crop last season, a pre-packaged salad and, of course, a bottle of red wine. With the corn slowly cooking on the stovetop, the lasagna in the oven and the salad ready for dressing in the bowl, he left to clean up for his special guest.

He remembered the night their universes collided. They gave in to their sexual needs. No holding back. They spent every free moment together the summer she graduated from high school and decided to try a long distance relationship when Cat started college at the University of Minnesota. By Halloween, their relationship was over.

He assumed the breakup had a lot to do with him being a farmer. He loved tending the land and watching what he planted grow, turning out a product his country needed. The land loved him back.

Now the question was—would Cat accept the proposal to be his wife?

Waiting for the guest of honor, he paced the length of the main hall between the kitchen and the master suite.

Blondie's bark announced Cat's arrival. Josef stepped onto the front porch. "Did you get done what ya needed to?"

"The house wasn't bad, considering." She tipped her head, her face etched with sorrow. "I cleaned enough for my week's stay." Cat bent and petted the yellow lab.

"If ya find it difficult to stay there, you're more than welcome here." He held the front door open and caught a whiff of the tropics as she entered the house. She wore jean shorts with multiple layers of tank tops.

"It smells wonderful. What are we having?"

"Lasagna, garlic bread, salad." The door closed. "Why don't ya sit down, relax, and I'll be right back."

"I didn't notice before, but you have a beautiful home. I don't remember the house looking like this when we were kids."

"I rebuilt it about four years ago. Tore the old place down and built from the ground up the way I wanted," he hollered from the kitchen and reappeared with two glasses of red wine. "For you." He handed her a glass. "Dinner should be ready in about fifteen minutes." The wine swirled around, clinging to the sides of the glass.

He contemplated whether to sit next to her or in the chair. The chair won since he didn't want to move in on her yet. Silence hung in the air like the swirls of the wine slowly sliding down the inside of his glass.

"Any luck finding another place for the horses?"

"No, but I have to now." She stared into the glass she held. "The land sold, and I have only forty-five days to remove the horses."

"Are you okay?" He leaned forward and rested his hand on her bare knee.

"I'll be fine." She looked where his hand rested.

He stood. "Why don't we check on dinner?" Cat followed him into the kitchen.

"Oh, my God. This is beautiful," she exclaimed. "You live here alone yet have double ovens, a six burning stove and an industrial 'fridge. Do you use all of this?"

"I like to cook on occasion and entertain the family. And just because I live on a farm doesn't mean I have to cook on a wood burning stove." They laughed as he pulled the bread from the upper oven and cut it into slices.

"I didn't mean—"

"I know, but we farmers are modern, too, and like nice things." He tossed the sliced bread into the basket. "Why don't ya go ahead and dish up while I get the salad ready."

"This looks good." Cat scooped a section of lasagna from the foil pan. "You worked all day making it I'm sure."

"Oh, yeah, all day," he jabbed back as he walked to the dining room, setting the salad bowl on the table. "Me and Stouffers." He entered the kitchen and filled his plate.

"It looks delicious, and I'm thankful. I love the counter tops. What are they made of?"

They sat at the mission style table. "Concrete. It's amazing all the different things they can do with it." Josef bowed his head to pray. When he lifted his head, brown eyes stared at him.

"No wonder Elaine liked you so. I remember going to church every Sunday, sitting and listening, not understanding a word of the Latin they spoke."

"I remember that, too, but it's all in English now." He lifted his wine glass. "How 'bout a toast—to Elaine and her eternal happiness." As their glasses clinked, a tear from the corner of her eye fell, and his knuckle gently touched her cheek to swipe it away.

* * * *

Catherine placed the last of their dinner dishes on the gray and black swirled countertop.

"Go sit in the living room, and I'll take care of this. I'll join ya in a minute." Josef loaded the dishwasher.

"Okay." She retreated to the living room, sat on the sofa and surveyed the room. The living room was much more than the living room Josef referred to. It was a great room. A man's room—leather, wood, stone and dark colors. Navy and wine throw pillows accented the deep evergreen leather sofa and chairs. The coffee table was a slab of rough-cut marble stone. Farm, hunting and health magazines littered the beautiful top. Blondie's big dog bed lay near the TV.

"You're smiling. That's a good sign."

She jumped at the sound of Josef's voice.

"Sorry." He sat beside her, and her heart stuttered.

"It's okay. I scare easily. I can see someone coming, go back to whatever I was doing, and when they approach and say something, I jump. It's stupid."

"Funny. Not stupid. I'll have to remember to announce myself."

"Can I see the rest of the house?" she asked, curious to see if the upstairs was anything like the main floor—modern, yet manly.

"Sure. I can't guarantee it'll be clean though." He stated with a brave smile, and she laughed.

"Would you mind if I had another glass of wine?"

"No, go ahead, and finish the bottle."

"That's okay," she sashayed into the dining room, "I don't need to drink three-quarters of a bottle."

"There's not much left," he chuckled.

She lifted the bottle, looked at the amount remaining and asked, "Did we drink that much with dinner?"

Catherine stood between the archway and foyer as Josef advanced. He wore a black short-sleeved polo shirt and khaki cargo shorts. She suspected he'd made an effort to look nice for her. Her jean shorts and tank tops came up lacking.

His shirt showed off muscular arms, and his legs weren't bad either. They weren't tanned like his arms, but built the same, which showed he cared about his body. She wondered what lay beneath the black shirt. "How about that tour now?" Her face heated with the thoughts.

"Well, you've seen most of the main floor." They cut through the dining room and crossed the hall.

His large, firm hand warmed her lower back, and her heart was at DEFCON Two—Defense Readiness Condition. Level Two—things are heating up. She pondered the earlier discussion they'd had about marriage, but quickly dismissed the thought.

"I have this office and off the kitchen there's a guest bathroom on one side of the hall and the laundry on the other side."

The office was a light tan color and had a futon covered with a dark brown and navy quilt.

"This is my room." He gestured to the door at the end of the hall. "I didn't spare anything with the master suite."

They entered through double doors. A suite indeed. To the right a king sized bed with a table on each side commanded the center of the large room. A wide dresser stood near the foot of the bed while an upright one stood against the main wall. The far wall had two sets of French doors leading to a patio off the back of the house.

"The bathroom." His hand swept to the left.

"Shit! This is as large as my bedroom."

There was a walk-in shower and a whirlpool bath, big enough for two. His and her sinks in the vanity and the toilet in its own little room. Also in the bathroom were his and her closets.

She caught him kicking clothes into a closet. "This is unbelievable. You did a fantastic job with the rebuild."

"Thanks. I'd like to think so. I've worked hard and plan to work harder." He stood in the doorway to the hall, leaning against the doorframe, gazing at her as she stood by his bed. Her heart rate accelerated, now at a DEFCON One—something is going to break loose at any second.

"Maybe it's time I see the upstairs." With caution, she approached the doorway. Her mind and body were in a battle of wants and needs.

The stairs led to a landing, which looked out to the front yard, and continued with several more steps leading to the second floor open hallway. She stepped forward and leaned over the rail, taking in the great room below.

"The house is so big, and you live here alone."

"Someday I'll find the right girl, and we'll fill the house with kids."

"Girl, huh?" She hip-checked him with a wink.

"You know what I mean."

"How many rooms are up here?"

"Four and two baths of sorts."

"Of sorts?"

"You'll see what I mean." He led her to the left down a short hallway.

She entered a nice sized room decorated for a girl. *Faery* came to mind with the walls painted in lime green and varying shades of purple accents.

"Here's the bathroom *of sorts*. It's like a Jack and Jill, but not."

The faery room had an attached room with a sink in it. They walked through a pocket door and the small room contained the toilet on one side and a shower on the other.

"I see what you mean. Not a true bathroom." She continued through another room with a sink and into a bedroom. "This is beautiful." The room was decorated with a feminine touch, white and pink shabby chic with a country motif.

"My sister-in-law thought it would be nice for any girl who stayed. The other side is the same but decorated for guys. Did you want to see them?"

"Yes."

They walked across the walkway to the other side of the house and the rooms *were* identical in layout.

"You weren't kidding. Makes it easy for the builder."

The smaller room at the front of the house was set up for a boy with sports themed paint in dark blue and green. The room to the back of the house was painted a light tan/brown with shades of aqua accents.

Walking downstairs Catherine said, "Thank you for letting me see the house. You did a good job."

At the bottom, Josef took her hand and turned her around. "Cat, have ya thought any more about the will and farm?"

She slipped her hand from his and turned to enter the great room. "Yes."

"And?"

"I'm still undecided."

"We've shared a lot in our past, Cat." Josef sat next to her on the leather sofa. "We may not have stayed in touch, but I have with your family." He held her hand in his. "Your great-aunt really adored you. You brought her so much happiness." He lifted her chin, and she met his gaze. "She loved you like a daughter. You know that?"

A tear trickled down her cheek, and she swiped it away. "Yes. But I don't understand why she didn't give me what I needed. And why the marriage trust fund."

"She knew about your love for animals and the need to help them. The only thing I can think of is that she thought the land would be of better use for you and the animals. More to work with. I don't understand it either. And well, the marriage thing, I have no answer."

She removed her hand from his. She was afraid. Afraid of what he might ask. Afraid of what she might say. Afraid of what she might do. "I don't have anyone in my life, so how could I get married?" The tears disappeared, as she grew more upset with the situation. "I've never had a relationship last longer than a month."

"We lasted longer than a month."

"We were kids." She looked to the wooden floor.

"No, Cat." His fingers gently lifted her face to look at him. "I was a man, and you were a woman."

"We used each other to satisfy a sexual need," she said matter of factly and sat upright. "When you weren't there, I found it elsewhere. The reason the long distance thing didn't last."

"Wow." His voice was toneless as he bowed his head.

"Sorry, but you brought it up." She fell back against the leather. "I thought you knew when I told you it wasn't working. That we were over.

I thought, well, I guess I should've been honest and up front with you."

Silence filled the room.

"We've both grown and learned as adults, Cat."

"It's getting late. I should leave." She stood and moved the short distance toward the front door. "I still have stuff to do tonight." A lie, but the conversation had become awkward.

Josef grabbed her hand, turning her into his chest and arms. She gazed into chestnut irises tinged with green.

"I'm here now, Cat."

Soft moist lips touched hers. She parted her lips as the kiss deepened. The sensation of his hands on her back and neck sent goose bumps across her skin as her head swirled with want.

She pulled away in an emotional fog. "I need to leave." Her fingertips touched her lips as though she could will away the kiss, but the fingers lingered for a moment.

"The past is in the past, Cat. Think about things. We could get married."

"I can't think about this right now." Catherine practically ran out the door for the old farmhouse.

Think about things? That's all she'd been doing.

Chapter Eight

Cat quickly crossed Josef's lawn toward Elaine's and peeked over her shoulder. Josef shook his head. Eleven years, and his body warmed the instant he kissed her. Did she feel the same thing? She must've. She'd allowed him to deepen the kiss.

He strolled through the house to the patio, Elaine's will on his mind with regard to its effect on Catherine. Why didn't Cat have a relationship that lasted longer than a month? Was she serious? Her mom had talked about how first school consumed Cat's life, then work and now her animal rescue.

The horses needed a new home. The farm would give her a place to put them. He had had every intention of proposing tonight but was thrown off when she mentioned cheating on him.

Josef lounged with arms folded behind his head. He didn't need the money Cat would get when she married, but he did want the land. Land that should be his. Not Cat's. He should've gotten it back in the will— without a marriage.

The story he heard growing up was real. About the poker game and the bet his great-grandfather put on the table. Neither he nor his family ever held a grudge against Cat's family. It became the tale to tell the children, grandchildren and on down the line. He never wanted the land as much as he did now though. Elaine leased the land to him. Desire for the land grew over the years, as did his understanding of why farming the land was important to his family and the world. He believed his destiny was to regain the land for his family. Gordon died, and Josef assumed, when Gordon and Elaine died childless, they would will it back to the Garrison family. With that option no longer plausible, he would do what needed to be done.

He'd get his land. Marry Cat, have it last long enough for her to receive the full trust fund rather than the church, get a divorce and get the land. She could have the farmhouse and buildings. One way or another, the land would be his.

* * * *

Sunday morning Catherine strolled to the barn. Opening the red wooden door, the strong smell of fresh hay engulfed her. Her senses came to life. She closed her eyes and inhaled deeply. The memory of children's laughter played in her mind. Eyes opened to see the rope hanging from the rafters where they would swing and drop into the hay piles.

Eyes down now, shuffling along the floor, she remembered the trap door that led into the stalls below. The well-worn iron ring was cold to the touch. She lifted the heavy door by the ring, letting it fall back with a thud on to the wood floor. Peering through the opening to the cement floor below, she missed the sounds of cows, pigs and chickens. Nothing but emptiness now.

Despite the silence, she heard something. And it wasn't her imagination.

Mewing from the haystacks. At the edge of the stacks, straining to hear for a sense of what direction to look, she climbed and moved to the left. There they were—a litter of kittens. She guessed them to be at least four weeks old. Mama cat wasn't around, probably out hunting for food. Catherine wouldn't intrude on the small family; however, she would periodically check on them.

Outside, she hopped down over the wood retaining wall where the slope was, as the barn was built into a hill. Although there were no cows, the aroma of manure was present when she strolled through the lower level of the barn. Her hand ran along the round metal gates of the cow stalls. This would've been the horses' new home. Saddened by the thought, she exited the barn.

She hustled up the slight incline, approached the swing and yanked the heavy ropes to test them. A little weight on the seat and a tight grip on the side ropes, in case the seat failed, she kicked out and set the swing in motion.

The old school bus parked by the shed caught her attention. She and the foster kids had played school in the thing for hours on end and take turns being the bus driver. Catherine smiled at the memory. They all loved pretending to drive and pull the lever to open the door, which would make the Stop sign pop out from the side.

Her legs pumped back and forth, propelling the swing higher and higher into the air. Then she let it slow and wondered again about Josef and marriage. If she married, she'd get the farm—and money too. Money would be nice but not necessary. The barn *was* necessary. She'd have a place to put the horses, and the dogs would have space to run, far more than her small townhouse offered. There were a lot of possibilities the farm could offer Four Hooves and Paws Rescue. But marriage?

The swing stopped, and she got off with a heavy sigh. Entering the kitchen, her stomach growled. The radio filled the quiet house with a little noise while she fixed a sandwich. A loud mechanical moaning came from the basement followed by a wet splashing. She jumped at the noise and cautiously walked to the basement stairwell door.

She didn't want to venture to a place she didn't like, not even to check out a strange noise. Opening the door, she flipped the light switch and peered down the stairs. Splashing. Water ran somewhere in the basement.

"Damn it," she exclaimed, slamming the door shut.

Her back rested against the closed four-paneled wood door. A battle raged in her mind.

You need to go and see what's going on.

No, I don't. Josef owns this now. It's his responsibility.

Just try to go down the stairs and get a better look.

"Fine, I'll go take a look." She turned, grabbed the clear glass doorknob and slowly opened the door as though a monster were going to jump out and attack. Her stomach knotted. Alone in the house, chances were she wouldn't find anyone dead down there, but it always came back to haunt her.

Through the open door, she placed a foot onto the first wooden plank. She swallowed the lump in her throat as her breath quickened. The other foot, another step. Her body trembled. Another step and a sickening wave of terror rocked through her body.

Catherine turned, racing back through the basement door and out the back screen door. Walking around the big oak, she breathed in and out until she could breathe through her nose. After the third lap, feeling calmer and more in control, she entered the house and grabbed her phone. She dialed and waited for Josef to answer.

"This is Josef. Leave me a message, and I'll get back to you."

"Josef, it's Catherine. I need your help. I'm sure the water heater went out because there's water in the basement. Come over ASAP." She sat at the kitchen table and finished her sandwich.

What was she going to do? No air conditioning was one thing, but no hot water was a different story. It appeared cold showers were in her future.

Gravel crunched from an approaching vehicle twenty minutes later. His truck pulled into the roundabout and parked behind her pickup.

Catherine met him on the steps. "I didn't expect you here so soon."

"Well, if there's water in the basement, ya don't have time to waste." Josef walked to the back of the truck and opened the tailgate. "I brought my pump to get the water out. Then we'll assess the damage."

Josef wiggled his way into water waders, put a bulky roll of tubing over his shoulder and grabbed the large pumping mechanism. "I'm assuming ya haven't gone down there yet?" He peered back at her.

"I tried, but I couldn't do it."

"What is it with you and that basement?" He set the pump on the ground. "Ever since you were little, you've never liked going down there. You afraid of the boogeyman getting you?" He chuckled, but she didn't find it funny.

"No. Maybe it's the steep narrow stairs, stone walls, dirt floor and lack of windows down there. I don't know. I get creped out."

"Well, let's get to work." Josef walked in and straight for the basement.

"What do you want me to do?" She followed as far as the top of the stairwell.

He turned on the second step and looked at her. "Come stay at my place." He stated it plain and simple, continuing down the wooden staircase and stepped into water. He turned with a stern face. "Shit,

Catherine! Why didn't you shut the water off?" and disappeared from sight.

She winced. It couldn't be helped. She tried going into the basement but couldn't. There was mumbling from the basement, but nothing clear could be made out because of the splashing. He probably cursed her with each step.

He came around the corner dropping an end of the black tubing in the water and unwound it up the stairs. In the narrow passageway, his chest brushed against hers, and their eyes held. A connection bore into her soul. Warmth swept over her body, while her nipples perked, exposed through the thin layers of her shirt. Something was there between them. He jogged down the back steps, she trailed behind, and he fired up the pump.

"I tried to go down, Josef. I just couldn't do it. I'm sorry," she yelled over the loud humming.

Water from the hose splashed onto the dry soil.

"It'll be fine," he stated irritated as he bent over the machine. Standing, he glanced at her and walked to his truck. "Pack your things and stay at my place." It was a statement rather than a suggestion.

"Why?"

"You'll need a place to stay." His tone softened as he slid the water waders off, an action she found oddly sexy.

"How long is this going to take?"

"Probably until tomorrow and you'll be without water. With a busted pipe, you can't do dishes, bathe or use the toilets. I shut the main water off. So why don't ya pack your bags and come stay at my place?" He tossed the waders into the back of the pickup.

"Thanks, but I'll be fine. I can eat out." Staying at his place would be too challenging for her wanting body.

"What about the bathroom?" He leaned against the tailgate.

"I'll take you up on using your facilities." Score one for Josef, pointing out the lack of bathroom facilities.

"Okay, suit yourself. But know the door is always open." Behind the truck's wheel, he added, "I'll be by to see how things are progressing."

Waving good-bye, she watched him drive away. *I'll be just fine.* The pump hummed loudly. The water gurgled and flowed through the tube as it made its way outside. The noise wore on her. She had to leave.

Catherine unleashed the dogs. "Come on, boys. Let's go for a ride." She held the door open to the pickup cab. Darby and Fuzzy jumped in. Fritz with his healing injury took a little time. "Should I go stay with Josef?"

Darby barked in response.

"I'm not sure that'd be a good idea."

She earned another response from the Lab.

"Why? If he were to kiss me again, I'm not sure I could back away. Nope, I think we'll stay where we are."

Fritz's head hung out the window with the wind blowing the fur from his face. His tongue hung out to the side. She giggled. The tension through her shoulders and back released. What's done was done. She laughed the situation away.

Approaching the business district, she slowed until she spotted the hardware store. "I'm going to see if Harvey's working the register." Pulling into the small parking lot, she put the windows part way up so the dogs couldn't hop out, but got the fresh air they needed.

The bell on the door clanged, the same bell from her childhood. The familiar, musty old smell hung in the air. A clean, fresh coat of paint brightened things though. The shelves were rearranged, but the front register looked the same, with the five and ten-cent candy sitting in the same spot.

Old man Harvey sat behind the register, and she smiled. "Harvey, how are you?" She approached the counter, and the bald-headed man stood.

Before she could remind him of who she was, he said, "Catherine Mornelli. My, how you've grown. You've got your mother's beauty."

"Oh, thank you," she said as warmth spread from her neck to her face. "You're looking good. How's business?"

"Slow but steady. Enough to stay in business. Is there something I can help you with today?" Harvey stepped from behind the counter.

"I stopped in to see you and check out the candy selection."

"You're such a nice girl. Sorry about Elaine. She was a special lady." Sadness crept over his face.

"Thank you. That means a lot." Catherine's gaze wandered over the selection of old time candy. "I love that you still have this stuff."

"Had to raise the prices. It's a little higher than what you'll remember spending as a kid."

"It's worth it." She put a box of Boston Baked Beans and a roll of assorted Necco Wafers on the counter and paid him a dollar fifty. "Thanks, Harvey. I may be back for another fix before I leave town."

He raised his hand in acknowledgment, and the bell rang overhead as she exited. The box of beans rattled in her hand as she approached the truck. The dogs wiggled at the sound.

"This isn't for you guys. It's my special treat." She opened the box and poured out a handful, popping a couple in her mouth. After sucking for a short moment, she crunched past the smooth candy-coated shell and through to the peanut. "Just like I remember."

All three dogs stared as though she were crazy.

"It tastes good," she said to them and tossed another handful into her mouth.

Catherine returned to the farm. With the dogs on their leashes, she grabbed the bag containing kitten food and bowls from the back of the truck. To avoid the loud obnoxious engine of the pump, she opened the barn door. The kittens mewed. Time to step in. Eagerly the kittens pushed each other at the bowls while they devoured the food. What happened to their mother? Did she leave in the hunt for food and get killed? Or did she just abandon them?

The bowls emptied, the kittens mewed in protest as she left.

"I guess you're mine now." She faced the six of them. "We'll need to set a few ground rules though." Careful not step on one of the tiny creatures, she continued outside.

"First rule, you will not be allowed into the house. You are barn cats and need to keep the mice away. Secondly, well, I guess there are no other rules. You own this farm, just not the inside of the house."

She set the bowls on the ground, sat on the swing and pumped her legs, mindful of the kittens. The kittens mewed for a short time and ventured about the yard. Catherine pumped her legs and with good momentum, the breeze she generated brought relief from the sticky humid air.

While in mid-air, she jumped off, stood, picked up the bowls and went into the house. She felt the grumble of her stomach. Dinner time.

No light shone from the interior of the refrigerator. No cool air escaped through the open door. She reached to grab the sandwich fixings—they were warm to the touch. Catherine slammed the door closed and yelled. "God, what else can go wrong?" She sank to the floor. "What am I going to do now?"

Chapter Nine

During a busy night at The Watering Hole, Josef found a spot in the farthest reaches of the parking lot. Her truck parked near the front of the lot led him to believe Cat had been there for a while. Music poured out as he opened the door. He paused a moment to let his eyes adjust to the darkness. In the back of the bar, a woman, obviously drunk, sang AC/DC's "You Shook Me All Night Long." Off key and too loud.

As he neared the stage and the back table where Wayne, Elliot and Jackson sat drinking, his mouth dropped opened. Cat stood behind the microphone, his buddies focused on her.

"How much has she had to drink?" He shouted above the noise as he slid onto the bench seat next to Jackson.

"Enough, I'd say," Elliot replied, not taking his eyes off Cat. "She sure did grow up."

"Back off! She's mine," Josef stated emphatically.

Cat looked over to their table, directly at him and wrapped up the song. With a disapproving shake of his head, she hopped off the stage and approached the table.

Before he could get out from the booth, she slid in close to him. "How long have ya been here?" He was concerned, not angry with her.

"I had some dinner and drinks." Her speech slurred as she spoke. "What would you guys say? Two hours or so?"

"She was sitting here eating when we arrived." Wayne gave Josef a wide-eyed, slight head tilt don't-blame-us-for-her-actions look.

"I saw Wayne and asked him to join me. It's been fun catching up. Then Elliot and Jackson came, and we got the party started." Cat snatched a fancy drink concoction from the table and slurped what was left in the glass.

Josef removed the drink from her possession. She sounded like a toddler drinking from a straw for the first time. "I think ya should slow down, Cat." She swayed in the bench toward the aisle. His arm wrapped around her to hold her in place.

"After the day I've had, I'd say I deserve another one." She raised her arm to gain Bridget's attention. "Better yet, I'll buy the table a round."

"I stopped by, and the water is almost gone." *A pipe bursting doesn't justify her drinking like this. What the hell?*

Bridget stepped to the table. "Hey, Joe," she sang. "Can I bring you the usual?"

"Hey, Bridge, you can bring the whole table a round on me." Cat leaned into Josef, her hand splayed on his chest before resting her head on his shoulder.

"How nice of you." Bridget gave a condescending glance to Cat. "Joe, the usual?" Bridget repeated with a wink. Was that jealousy in her voice?

"Yeah." Josef snickered at the two women and their lack of acknowledgement of each other. "Thanks, Bridget."

"When did you stop by? Oh wait, it had to be *after* the refrigerator died on me."

"The 'fridge died?" Maybe *now* she would stay at his place. No hot water and no refrigerator could make things uncomfortable and inconvenient.

"I just said that."

"Okay. Why don't ya sing another song? I want to talk to the guys—alone." He didn't mind her making a fool of herself singing. It was a fact she was drunk though he would keep her from drinking anymore.

"Why?" she asked in a drunken whine.

"Why what?"

"Why do you need to be alone to talk to the guys? I'm like one of the guys."

"Do you know about tractors and farming?"

"No." She pouted like a toddler, which paired well with her straw drinking abilities. He chuckled.

"Have fun, and sing a song."

"I'll go see what else they have." She stumbled off the bench, and Josef gave her a pat on the butt. "You devil you." She turned, winked and approached the stage.

"I bought a ring Friday," Josef said when Cat was out of earshot perusing the song list.

"You're getting married for a farm? Jesus, Joe. I don't believe it."

"Jackson," Josef leaned into the center of the table, "if *I* don't marry Cat, I lose my great-grandfather's land to her. I'll do whatever it takes not to let that happen."

"Whatever it takes?"

"Whatever it takes. I made the decision we'll stay married for five years before I divorce her. That way she'll get the full trust fund and not lose the money to the church."

Cat's voice sang the opening lyrics to Prince's "I Would Die 4 U." If that's what you wanted to call the noise coming from the stage.

"Five years is a long time. Anything could happen," Elliot stated.

"Yeah, you two could have a couple of kids by then," Wayne chimed in.

"I'm not planning on kids, and she'd better not plan on it either."

"Drinks, guys." Bridget stepped to the table. "Joe, I think your *friend* could use your help. She stepped outside and didn't look so good."

"Thanks. Put this on my tab, Bridget. I don't think we'll be back." He slid from the booth. "See you Tuesday night."

Josef stepped into the neon-lighted night but didn't see her out front. He turned the corner to the parking lot as a deep voice said, "Come on, babe, shake me all night long," followed by a retching sound.

"Cat," he approached her and the man hovering over her. "I've got her, buddy. You can go back to the party inside."

"No, the party for two is back at my place. You go back inside."

Josef stood tall, grabbed the guy's arm and yanked him away from Cat. "She's with me, and *you* need to leave"

"Ooh, big man. Fuck you!" The guy swung and missed. Josef planted a fist in the man's stomach, and he doubled over to his knees.

"Cat, come on. Let's get ya home." Holding her by the waist, they staggered to his truck, and he helped her in.

"My hero," she said as he started the pick-up. "You saved me again."

"Again?" He glanced at her slumped in the seat.

"What would I've done without you and all that water?"

"Oh." He reached over her, pulled and fastened the seatbelt.

"I'm leaving tomorrow."

"Don't leave."

"God's sending me a message, and that message is to leave."

He drove onto Main Street, and they rode in silence until turning onto the dirt road for home.

"Ya need to sleep things off. You're staying at my place tonight. You can get a warm shower in the morning and a hot breakfast."

"Can I get anything else?" She squeezed his thigh.

"Cat." He removed her hand before his body could react. "As much as I wouldn't mind, I'm not taking advantage of you in the state you're in."

"What state is that? I'm in Minnesota just like you." She laughed at her own joke, and he smiled.

"You've been drinking." He pulled into his drive, put the truck in Park and assisted her out.

"I feel better now that I threw up in the parking lot."

"Let's get ya inside and into bed." He stayed by her side in case of a misstep.

"I like the sound of that." Her arms wrapped around his waist as she stumbled.

"Whoa, I've got ya." He opened the back door, and Blondie greeted them. "We've got company tonight, girl." The dog barked, and Josef held the door for the Lab to go out.

"Come on, Joe. Make my day better." She slid one hand down to his crotch.

He stopped her. "Marry me," he blurted, thinking aloud. He wanted to ask her tonight, but this wasn't how. He knew she was aware enough to know what was happening, and they had talked about it before.

She removed her arms, stood straight, bracing herself against the doorframe of the kitchen. "You're serious?" she slurred.

"Hang on." He darted into the dining room. Opening the china cabinet drawer, he grabbed the black velvet box and returned to the kitchen.

Cat sat with her head in her hands at the dining table. He approached with caution and bent to one knee. "Cat?"

She removed the hands cradling her face.

"Will you marry me?"

"Oh, my God. You *are* serious." She pushed the chair away from the table. "I … I …"

"Will you put the ring on? Ya don't have to give me an answer yet. But will ya put the ring on and wear it while you're here. You can give me your answer before you leave."

Silence.

His heart hammered against his chest.

He opened the box and pulled the simple one-carat round cut diamond set in silver from the box. With no rejection yet, he slid the ring on her finger. It fit. Perfectly.

"Cat?" He lifted her chin to see her brown eyes.

"Yes."

"Yes, you'll marry me, or yes, you'll wear the ring?" He couldn't read her mood or tone.

"Yes, I'll marry you." She gazed at the ring.

"You won't regret this." His thumb caressed her knuckles.

"I need to go." She stood, swayed and regained her balance. "I need to think."

He blocked her exit. "Think about what? You want to get married right?"

"I need to think." She stepped around and staggered out the front door.

"Cat," he called marching after her. "Stop."

She did just that, bent over and heaved more of the night's drinks on his drive. The dogs barked from across the road.

"I need to feed the dogs."

"Don't leave like this. Let's talk."

"Talk? About what?" She remained bent over. "You're right. I need to sleep this off."

"You're staying here." Hands around her waist, he helped her toward the house. "You'll get a warm shower and breakfast, too."

"Why?"

"Ya don't have water or a refrigerator," he chuckled, opening the door.

"No. Why did you ask me to marry you? There's nothing in it for you."

Watch yourself. "I'm not married, and you need rescuing. I'm your hero. Remember?"

"I remember." She enfolded him in a hug.

"Okay, let's get ya to your room. I'll take care of the dogs after I find you a toothbrush and shirt to sleep in."

They took the stairs one at a time.

"Can I sleep in the shabby chic room?"

"The what?" He didn't understand women and their design names.

"The pink and white room."

"Oh. Yeah. That's where I was planning on putting you." They turned the corner to the room where he propped her against the wall. "I'll be right back." He went downstairs to his room to get a shirt. With no luck finding a toothbrush, he returned upstairs.

As he came around the corner of the bedroom, she stood on the balcony wearing her bra and underwear. She turned with mischief in her brown eyes.

He went to the bathroom, found a toothbrush, and when he turned to go back into the room, she blocked his exit.

"Here's a new toothbrush." He struggled not to touch her as she took it from him. "You'll find toothpaste in the drawer." His body responded to a need she could fulfill. He held out the undershirt in his hand. "You can sleep in this."

She took his hand instead of the shirt. "Take me in your bed, Joe," and placed his hand on her moist mound. "I want you. I know you want me." She leaned against his chest and rubbed against his hardness. "And now we're engaged."

Oh God, she's going to drive me insane. "Cat—"

"Joe?" She purred in his ear like the cat she was.

He cleared his throat and choked out, "Not tonight." He removed himself from her and the bathroom. "I'll see you in the morning."

He strutted through the hall as best he could and at the landing of the stairs, he adjusted his jeans for the swollen state of his manhood. Her bedroom door slammed closed. Yeah, the sex would've been good, if not better than what he remembered, but he couldn't do it. He wanted her aware of him and every touch he placed on her body. He wanted to see her reactions. He wanted her to hear every sound she made and every sound he made. He wanted her but with no regrets.

* * * *

The sun fought through the sheer covered vertical blinds and beamed her square in the eye. Catherine rolled, pulling the covers up and groaned. *Sheets and cool air? Where?* Through squinted eyes, she remembered she stayed at Josef's place.

"What time is it?" she asked the empty room and rolled to the other side looking for a clock. No luck. "Ugh, my head."

She sat on the edge of the bed, and the sun caught the diamond engagement ring. Splashes of tiny rainbows sparkled as she stared at her hand. "Oh. My. God! What did I do last night?"

A rhetorical question. She *always* remembered her actions when drunk. Sometimes that was a good thing and other times, not so good. Her head thumped in agony. *Should've stuck to drinking beer.* Did she make the right decision? Better yet, did Josef know what he was asking? *He had a ring. Of course, he knows what he was doing.* She had to leave his house and think.

Catherine opened the bedroom door, listened and stepped into the bathroom. She changed into her clothes, grabbed her shoes and stood by the railing. Scanning the great room below, she heard not a sound of life in the house. She dashed down the stairs, out the front door and headed for Elaine's.

Safe.

The dogs barked with joy as she collapsed on the back stairs and caught her breath. "Give me a minute, guys, and then I'll fill your bowls."

Fritz strolled up with his tail wagging. "How you doing, big fella?" She rubbed his back and checked the wound site. "Looking good. Don't worry. The hair will grow back." She scratched his lower back end. Fritz wiggled his butt from side to side. "Oh, does that feel good?"

"All right. Time to feed you and the kittens." She went inside, filled the dogs' bowls and grabbed the kittens' bowls before going to the barn.

"Here kitty, kitty, kitty. I have food for you."

The litter mewed.

"I'll be back for the bowls. And stay out of trouble." With all six accounted for, she left them to eat.

Back in the kitchen, she remembered why she had decided to stay at Josef's. "I have no food or hot water. I can't go back over there. Not yet." She glanced at the ring on her finger.

Locating her computer bag, Catherine sat on the front porch step. While the laptop fired up, she gazed at the rising sun, closed her eyes and appreciated the warmth it delivered. With pressure on her lap, her eyes opened to a grey and white fur ball sitting on her keyboard.

"Oh, no, you don't." She grabbed the small ball of fluff off and sat the kitten next to her leg. "That is one place you can't go. You stay right here."

The kitten mewed in response.

She stroked the fur of her newfound friend and thought about the proposal, last night, the will and Josef. The kitten's motor purred. With each stroke, Catherine relaxed a little more.

"Fluffy, that's your name. Being that I don't know your sex yet, it's the perfect unisex name."

Fingers stroked the keyboard and petite rainbows from the diamond ring caught her eye. She typed in 'MN marriage license.' With a few more clicks she had her answer. Five days. Five days after applying for a license she could be married.

"Well, no need to worry about being married within the will's ninety day time frame." She shut down the laptop and went into the house.

Hungry but nothing to eat, she grabbed for keys and stopped. "Damn. My truck's at The Watering Hole." She sighed in resignation. "I have to go to Josef's."

Chapter Ten

A fitful night of sleep proved Josef's early morning wake-up a difficult task, but he took care of chores before returning to the house. With no life in the kitchen or living room, he went to the room she slept in. The door stood open. He stared into nothingness at the reality—Cat was gone. Did she leave the ring behind, or were they still getting married. He blinked rapidly and hustled to the bathroom. She didn't shower, and no ring lay on the counter.

There was hope for a wedding after all. His heart beat a little faster.

In the kitchen, he glanced at the countertops. No ring. Warmth spread through his heart. She still wore the ring. Did she leave, embarrassed by her behavior last night? Nah, not Cat. Maybe she ate and went to feed the dogs. Damn, maybe she's having second thoughts? He opened the refrigerator to make lunch, reminding him Cat's fridge was broken. *She's got to be hungry.* Lunch out would give them the opportunity to talk about marriage. Without her making a scene.

Out the back door, he crossed the road and spotted her standing on the back steps of Elaine's house. "Cat," he yelled as he stretched into a light jog. She turned in acknowledgement. "Let's grab some lunch and talk before picking up your truck."

"You may not want to come any closer." Her hand stopped him. "I should probably shower first. Do you mind?"

"Nope. Grab your things and come on over. We'll go when you're ready." He smiled as she disappeared in the house to get clean clothes and stuff for her shower.

She opened the door. "I was just headed your way." The wave of her hands gestured him to start moving. "Josef, is this for real? Are we really getting married?"

"We'll talk later," he stated a few steps ahead of her. "I'm hungry."

The wait for Cat to shower didn't take long, and they were on their way. Bright sun filled the cab, and Cat's black hair reflected a sleek shine. He glanced to her hands where she twisted the ring around her finger, as though contemplating her decision.

"What are you hungry for?" He focused back to the road in front of them.

"Let's go to The Watering Hole."

"I'd rather not." It escaped as a bit snide, and he swallowed the lump that formed in his throat.

"Why? Did I embarrass you last night?"

"No, but as you said, we were just there. How does pizza sound?" He didn't want questions by the staff at The Watering Hole. They knew him all too well. Leaving with Cat last night would raise more questions.

"Fine." It came out like a submissive whatever-you-say-but-I'd-rather-have-something-else fine. The kind of *fine* a woman says when it's not fine.

On the main road, he drove the short distance to Pizza Hut and glanced at her. "It looks nice." She continued playing with the ring.

He parked the truck, while an awkward silence vibrated in the air. Once he killed the engine, he turned and took her hand in his. "Cat, will you marry me?"

"Yes." She leaned in and kissed him gently on the lips. "Yes, I'll marry you." The apprehension in her voice couldn't be missed.

"It'll be okay." He released her hand. "Let's go in."

Once seated at a table, he would wait to bring up wedding arrangements until after they ordered.

"We have to wait a minimum of five days after applying for a marriage license before the wedding," she said, then picked up her menu and hid her face as though seeking shelter.

So much for waiting to approach the subject. "You've looked into it then." This surprised him because of her lack of enthusiasm about the whole idea.

"This morning. Can I move forward with barn renovations?" She showed emotion at last. Concern. Not the emotion he wanted her to have, but an emotion nonetheless.

"Of course."

She set the menu down and played with the napkin-wrapped silverware. Something bothered her.

He took her hand in his with hopes of soothing away her worries. "I'd like to be married at St. Michael's and have Father Tim officiate. I think there are classes we have to take." The church played a major role in his life, and there was no other place he'd rather get married.

"You talk to Father since you know him. I need to take care of other things." She removed her hand from his and twisted a section of hair.

"What do ya need to take care of?" He struggled to understand why she pulled away and distanced herself.

"I have a life back in the cities to figure out," she said disagreeably. She averted her eyes by glancing out the window then at the tabletop. Anywhere but watching his reaction.

"Okay, no need to be snotty." He would approach further discussion about their marriage carefully.

They sat in silence until the pizza arrived. Her fingers worked the same strand of hair repeatedly around one finger. If her eyes made contact with his, they immediately darted in another direction. He didn't understand her behavior.

"We can move ya into the house when you're ready. I know you work, but know you don't have to if ya don't want to." They each took a bite. He picked up his slice while she used a fork.

"I could commute."

Josef coughed on a bite. "You're kidding?" How could she be serious about commuting between work and Oak City?

Her brown eyes connected with his. "No," she stated in a definite determined voice.

"I just thought you'd find work here or focus on your rescue thing."

"Well, you thought wrong." Agitated, her mouth opened and snapped around the bite on her fork like a walleye taking a baited hook.

"I'm sorry." He'd better stop assuming with her and ask questions, or they'd never walk down the aisle. And right now, they both needed this marriage.

She finished chewing a bite. "What are your plans with the house?"

"What house? Mine's fine the way it is."

"Not your house, my Aunt Elaine's." Her voice radiated irritation while her eyes widened with the unspoken words *you're such a moron.*

He hadn't thought about the house. His only interest was the land. "I don't know. I hadn't thought much about it."

She shoved a forkful of their deep-dish meat lover's pizza in her mouth.

"When are ya going to tell your mom?" Josef took a long pull of pop from the straw. Although irritated, he continued to ask about their marriage. He gazed across the table at her but kept his smile to himself. Still stubborn and feisty.

"Tell her what?"

To prevent himself from spewing his drink all over her, he swallowed with a small choke. "*What?* That you're getting married. Aren't you going to tell them?"

"Yes, I'll tell them. I just don't know when. Can we keep it quiet for a while? You can talk to Father and start the process there. But I don't want anyone to know." She took another bite.

"You're wearing the ring. People will ask."

"I'll deal with it then." She played with a strand of hair.

He tipped his head down at his plate, not sure how she would take what he was about to say next. "My family and the guys know." He wanted *everyone* to know. Making it public would make it more difficult for her to back out of the wedding.

"Shit! So much for secrecy."

"I told them I was going to propose. No one knows you've said yes. I hoped you'd be here for the Fourth of July so we could celebrate with my family."

"I don't know. Let's finish, then take care of the marriage license before getting my truck."

He nodded in agreement.

"You have your driver's license, and we'll need a hundred and fifteen in cash. I'll pay for half, but need to hit a cash machine first," Catherine said politely.

"I'll take care of the cost. We go to the courthouse, right?" He picked up his crust and made short work of it in two bites.

"Yes, and you don't have to pay for it all." Cat finished her pizza and pushed her plate back.

"Soon enough my money will be your money and vice versa. So I'll pay." He had to be careful not to allude to the fact he wasn't in this marriage for the long haul. He paid for lunch and worked on finishing the last piece of pizza.

"Fine. You can pay for the license." There was that womanly agreement tone again. "As for our money situation, what's mine is mine and will be used for Four Hooves and Paws Rescue." She twisted the drink straw between her finger and thumb.

"Okay, we'll see how things work out that way. Which I'm sure will be fine. Now if you're not leaving, come stay at my place. The dogs are welcome, too."

"Thank you. So … the earliest we could be married is next weekend. I'll leave you to talk to the church."

"Did ya want to get married next weekend? I'll check with Father when I talk to him." Moving on the marriage quickly would secure the will and land.

"Can we talk about this later?" Her tone and demeanor had softened.

"Yeah." He signed the receipt and followed her to the truck.

What was going on in that pretty little head of hers? Maybe she had come around to understand this marriage would benefit them both. With her acceptance of his proposal, maybe the moment for her to take the lead had arrived. Timing was of the essence, and Cat was smart enough to know how much she had before losing the trust fund.

Josef wished he could read her mind. Not knowing what she was thinking bothered him.

Chapter Eleven

After filing for the marriage license and picking up her truck, Catherine returned to Elaine's farm and thought about her life, wedding, Josef, work, Josef, marriage, Josef, work. And not necessarily in that order. As she fed the kittens, the decision was made. Time to pack up and stay at Josef's.

She drove across the dirt road and up his driveway. Blondie ran to her, tail wagging and barked in acknowledgment. "Hey, girl." She rubbed the Lab's back. "Where's Josef?"

"Rrr-ruff," Blondie responded.

"Oh, really. Let's go get him." Blondie darted from her side to the large shed where she barked and danced in and out of the open doors.

Loud rock music poured through the opening as she approached. There sat Josef in a large green machine. What the hell was it? *I don't recall Uncle Gordy ever having something like that.*

Blondie barked. Catherine jolted back to attention and walked beside a hulk of a tire and the edge of an attached ladder. "Josef," she yelled.

He jerked his head around. "Cat," he hollered in surprise, "just a second." The music stopped, and he climbed down the steps.

"I didn't mean to interrupt," she said as he hopped down. "What is this thing?"

"You're not interrupting. To put it simply, this is a combine."

The dirty overalls couldn't hide his muscular legs.

"It's huge."

"What brings ya by? And I know it isn't to learn about farm

equipment."

"I've decided to stay here. Where do you want me to chain up the dogs?"

His hands slid into pockets. "Good. Put the dogs where you'd like. Blondie can go wherever." Josef looked to his wrist.

Cat laughed. "What are you looking at?"

"What time is it?"

She checked her watch. "Almost five-thirty."

"How about dinner? Let me get in the shower, then I'll get cooking."

"Can I do anything to help?"

"When ya get the dogs and your belongings taken care of, if you want to see about starting up a vegetable and some baked beans, that would help."

"Okay." Catherine left the barn and returned to the truck for the dogs. She strolled around the yard and staked the chains in various locations so the dogs wouldn't get tangled together yet could play with Blondie.

Unpacking in the white and pink chic room, she thought about life back in the cities. She had to notify her boss she was leaving, deal with selling the townhouse and her belongings and then, of course, take care of the horses.

"Ya all settled in?"

Startled, she jumped at the sound of his deep voice. "Yeah, thanks."

He wore black cargo shorts and a tee shirt, which clung to his chest. His hair was still damp from his shower. He approached and pulled her near. Their bodies caressed. Her heart picked up a beat. Spices inundated her senses. For a moment, she paused to look at his oval face and full lips. Full-moist-kissable-lips.

His mouth connected with hers. When her legs bent, his large warm hand slid to her lower back, and he held her tight against his chest. His tongue probed. Her hand skimmed his arm to the wet hair where her fingers mingled and played.

The intensity of the kiss proved there was still a passion between them. Maybe this would work. Maybe it wouldn't be so bad. He broke away first. She was warm with want.

"We'd best start cooking." Catherine removed her hand from his hair. "Dinner, that is."

Catherine bowed her head as Josef said the prayer before they ate at a table on the patio. A loaded burger on her plate, along with the grilled corn on the cob, baked beans, and potato salad looked delicious.

"I was going to approach you the day the water heater and fridge went out about your earlier mention of marriage." She took a bite of burger.

"Really?"

"Hmmm," was the best she could do with a mouthful.

"Why? Do you really need the money?" He took a quarter bite size of his burger.

"I'd be lying if I didn't say I couldn't use it. More for the horses than for me. The money will help pay for the barn renovation and the cost of running Four Hooves and Paws."

They both took bites before she asked, "What's in it for you? Why do you want to marry me?"

"You wanted the barn, and the money will benefit you. I'm not interested in the money. The marriage allows me to continue farming the land without a fee. So, like you, I'd be lying if I said there was no benefit in it for me."

It remained silent for a moment as they ate.

"I believe Elaine knew exactly what she was doing when she wrote the will." Josef took a drink of water.

"What are you talking about?" She gave him a shocked look.

"You and I know she has tried to get us back together. Hell, your mother's even tried."

"My mother?" she exclaimed at his accusation.

"I've thought a lot about this. I think Elaine purposely gave us the opposite of what she knew each of us wanted and needed and put the trust fund based on marriage in the will to get us to work together and marry."

Her mouth hung open. She didn't care if she exposed chewed food. "Oh. My. God. I think you're right."

A section of hair spun around her finger. Her fork fell to her plate.

"My mom is in on this. I know it. When I questioned the amount of money in the trust fund, she told me not worry. That my Aunt Elaine was a perceptive businesswoman. My mom has money invested in this marriage thing."

"But how would she know a marriage would happen between you and me? You could've had a boyfriend or already been married. They didn't know when Elaine was going to die."

"Wills can change at any time. My mom's involved." She shoved the last of her food in her mouth and chewed with more force than needed.

"Does it matter?" His hand covered hers. "Does it change the situation?"

"No." He watched her. "No, it doesn't change things. I'll still marry you." Catherine picked up her plate and walked through the house to the kitchen.

Josef followed and set his plate on the counter behind her. His other arm came around to her other side. Trapped against the counter, she turned to face him.

"What are you doing?" she asked briskly as her face grew warm.

"I thought maybe we could pick up where we left off earlier in the bedroom. I felt the spark." He leaned in and warm lips met hers.

She pulled back. "We have more to talk about."

"Let's talk later. After …" he kissed her lips, "we …" nibbled her ear, "reignite …" lingered over a kiss on her neck, "our relationship," then returned to kiss her mouth as she melted into a puddle.

Her heart raced rapidly. Her stomach quivered. Her legs turned to jelly in the most delicious way.

As Josef pulled away, her eyes opened. He lifted her in his arms and exited the kitchen, passed the stairs and entered the master suite. He bent, laying her on the bed. His bed. He loomed over her with his hands at her sides. Nerves heightened and prickled like when your foot is asleep and you're trying to wake it up. Not knowing whether this was the thing to be doing or not, her body knew what it wanted. Its name was Josef.

The tee shirt clinging to his torso needed to come off. She grabbed the hem and pulled the shirt over his head. *Oh … my … God!* She tossed the shirt to the floor. Her hands wandered over his hairy chest.

He straddled her, trapping her arms with her shirt, giving him an advantage. He placed long succulent kisses across her breastbone, and she relished the moment. She wiggled out of her shirt, free now to touch his body. Her hands glided to his waistband where her fingers nimbly worked to free him of his shorts.

He stopped her progress and inched back for access to remove her shorts. Trailing kisses from her belly button to her breasts, he confiscated her bra. His tongue teased the first nipple. She arched her back at the sensation of his tongue and hand exploring her body. His fingers probed the warmth between her thighs, and she gasped.

Catherine pushed Josef's shoulder so he rolled to his back. Her hands made quick work removing his shorts and underwear. His length in her hand, she stroked his engorged manhood and straddled him.

Their bodies caressed. She wanted him more than she thought possible. Sliding up his shaft, her breasts grazed his chest and he snatched a breast in his mouth. She moaned his name, needing and wanting him. Slowly, she slid over him, wrapping her warmth around his length.

He released her breast, moaned her name and grabbed her hips.

He felt so good. So right. Every movement she made rocked her world.

Their bodies moved to an adagio tempo until their release, and she collapsed on top of him. Her heart hammered against his chest. Her ear rested over his beating heart.

Catherine moved so she was lying beside Josef, satisfied emotionally and sexually. Exhausted, she fell asleep in his arms.

Morning light peaked through wood blinds, and her eyes opened to find Josef gone. Up on her elbow, she found the clock. Six twenty-two. He was already at work.

For some reason she didn't want to bring sex into their relationship until after they were married. But they had history, so why not have sex? She didn't regret a minute of their tryst last night. If they weren't careful though, she could get pregnant.

She sat up, straight and rigid, at the reality of her last thought.

They hadn't used protection last night.

I could be pregnant.

Her heart hammered against her ribs. Her ears pounded. Breathing became difficult.

No, God wouldn't do that to her. Would He? Not after everything that happened in the last two weeks. Bad things happen in three's. First, there was the news about having to move the horses. Second, Elaine's death brought on the will and her wishes. *Third ... Third ... There's got to be a third.*

She rolled over, lying on her side, curled in the fetal position. She wanted to throw up. What had she done? What's the third bad thing?

After much thought, Catherine remembered the water heater and refrigerator. *That's it! That's the third.*

The realization made her nervous. Not necessarily a bad thing for her, but for Josef, she rationalized. No, it was the third because she was going to marry Josef.

Relief settled over her with the decision made about getting married. She would tell her family when she returned to the cities.

The waiting game to find out if she was pregnant started today. It would remain on her mind until her next cycle arrived. She closed her eyes thinking and counting days in her head. A little over a week and she'd know whether she was expecting or not.

Chapter Twelve

While together for breakfast and lunch, Cat remained quiet and spent the rest of the day at Elaine's. Josef gave her space. He'd scheduled his meeting with Father Tim to happen prior to poker with the guys at The Watering Hole.

He pulled into the empty church lot, parked and walked to Father's chancellery. He stepped through the door where the secretary greeted him and told him to go in.

"Josef, how are you?" Father extended his hand, and they shook in greeting.

"Fine, Father."

"Please sit down." He gestured to a simple upright chair situated in front of his desk. "So you want to talk about marriage classes. I didn't know you were engaged."

Josef maneuvered to get comfortable in the stiff chair. "I asked her to marry me this weekend, and she said yes. We'd like to be married here at St. Michael's. I know classes are required."

"Yes, they are. Who's the lucky lady?" Father sat comfortably in his chair.

"Catherine Mornelli."

The look on Father's face was priceless—wide-eyed and mouth agape. He instantly went rigid.

"As you know, we need to be married by mid-August."

"I'm sorry." Father's head shook. "I can't marry you two."

"Why not?" Josef's voice rose in anger. First Catherine gave him grief about the marriage and now Father Tim?

"This is not a marriage of love, but a marriage of convenience. The church will not condone such a thing," Father smirked with superiority as Josef's blood boiled.

"Who are you to say whether we are in love or not?" His hands balled in and out of fists.

"You know as well as I about Elaine's will and its content. Any marriage involving Catherine Mornelli is a farce."

Josef stood, leaned on Father's dark mahogany desk and stared into green eyes. "It is not a farce," he growled, "and we will be married. Catholic or not Catholic, there will be a wedding."

He stormed from the office, slamming the door shut, and growled at the secretary, "Have a nice evening." The raging storm continued to his pick-up. He sat in the truck's cab, slammed the steering wheel while red anger erupted.

"I should've known he wouldn't marry us. He wants the money. Damn it!" He slammed the wheel again, started the pick-up and headed to the poker game.

* * * *

Wayne, Elliot and Jackson sat in the usual booth. He walked by the bar and yelled to Bridget, "Shot of tequila and the usual."

"What the hell's wrong with you? Tequila?" Wayne slid over so Josef could sit.

"I'll tell ya after my shot." Bridget arrived with his shot and beer. "Thanks." He slammed the tequila down followed by a shake of his head. "Agh, good shit."

"So what gives? Does it have anything to do with Sunday night?" Elliot wiggled his eyebrows.

"You could say that." Josef took a long pull from the beer bottle to wash away the sting of the tequila.

"Didn't score, huh? Too bad." Jackson tossed back a swig of his beer.

"Depends on how ya look at it. For me, I scored and big. But that's not my problem. Father Tim is."

This earned him confused looks all around.

"I asked Cat to marry me Sunday night, and she said yes."

"Whoo-hoo," they all cheered.

Jackson slapped his shoulder. "You lucky dog. So when's the wedding?"

"Don't know. Hoped to be married at the church, but Father said he won't do it."

"You're shitin' us, right?" Wayne asked.

Josef took another pull of his beer. He deserved his wedding to be at St. Michael's. Raised Catholic, receiving every rite of passage and attending church every Sunday, he had earned it. But Father had him on it being a farce. He had loved Cat once, but the love wasn't there now. At least that's what he kept telling himself, arguing with his heart. And losing the battle more every minute.

"Nope." Josef explained what transpired in Father's office and finished with, "Hence the tequila."

"I don't blame you," Wayne consoled. "You can still get married by the JP."

"That's the only way we'll be able to." Josef slammed down the empty beer bottle and signaled for another. "Enough of this talk, let's play some poker."

* * * *

Josef glanced at Cat sitting in his pick-up. "You're not nervous, are ya?" he asked with sincerity.

"A little. It's been a long time since I saw everyone." She stared out the passenger window. "Do they all know?"

"Yes." He placed his hand on her leg. "They're happy for us. Relax."

No words were shared, but the emotions were. Strong emotions for both parties involved.

He kept his distance after their night together and wondered if he hadn't made a mistake. He had to focus on why he was marrying Cat. He wanted the land, and she needed the barn and money. Love wasn't part of his plan while sex would be a bonus. With sex came responsibility. They needed to talk about children. He knew where he stood on the topic, but what about Cat.

"Adam and David are married with no kids yet." He drove south toward the cities. "Adam and Maureen are expecting though. David's married to Marlene, Maureen's twin sister. John's dating Tiffany."

"Who married first, Adam or David?"

"David. But Adam and Maureen were dating first and the longest." A moment of silence and he asked, "Did you bring a swimsuit?"

"I didn't bring one with me when I packed for the farm."

"Do ya want to stop in North Branch to look for one?"

"Thanks, but I'll be fine." She glanced in his direction with the slightest smile.

"Okay. Maybe one of the girls will have something you could borrow. Sometimes they leave some at Mom and Dad's for spares."

"We'll see." She looked out the passenger window.

Was something bothering her? Something other than seeing his parents? Should he apologize for not talking to her after their night? No, it was in the past. Was she having second thoughts about the marriage? No, or she would've said something, and they wouldn't be going to his parents for the holiday.

He drove west of Cambridge and headed to the east side of Green Lake. The tree lined drive came into view. Cars filled the driveway. Blondie perked up first from the back of the truck's cab with Fuzzy, Darby and Fritz popping up to see where they were.

"This is nice." Catherine peered through the windshield.

"They wanted a place centrally located for the family." He parked next to Adam's Honda Ridgeline. "Dad liked the idea of being on the lake for fishing, and Mom enjoys it because the family loves to come here."

Before he opened the door, he added, "Don't worry about the dogs. My parents love Blondie. She's the only grandchild they have so far. They'll be happy to have more around."

Cat grabbed the dog leashes.

"Cat, let them run. They'll stay close to you or Blondie."

"No," she stated simply. "Okay, boys. We're here," and let them out of the back.

The dogs yanked her to the yard's edge where they marked their territory before going to the front door where he and Blondie stood waiting.

"Are ya ready?" With her nod he said, "There's nothing to be nervous about. You know my family." He turned the doorknob and held the door open for Cat and the dogs. The dogs tore into the house. Blondie led the pack, while Cat struggled to keep her dogs under control.

"Let them go. I promise it'll be fine. You can chain them outside."

Cat surveyed the furnishings.

"They can't hurt a thing. Let them check out things."

"Fritz, Darby, Fuzzy," she called out. The three came to attention, and she unclipped the leashes. "Behave," she informed them with a firm voice.

Cat stood as the dogs raced off, and Josef embraced her. "Relax." He delivered a quick kiss. "Let's go find everyone."

He led her through rooms to the back deck of the house with a beautiful view of the lake. Sure enough, everyone was in or by the water. He clasped her hand and descended the stairs when she suddenly stopped.

"What about the dogs?"

"What about them? They're in the house. They're fine. Relax." He continued down the stairs.

"You made it." Barbara, his mother, met them at the bottom of **the** stairs wearing her sparkling festive Fourth of July designed top with red pants. "Where are my grandkids?"

He hugged his mother. "They're in the house. Nice to see you, too."

"Catherine, how are you?" Barbara stepped from him and pulled Catherine into her arms. "I'm so sorry about Elaine's passing. She was a great friend and neighbor."

"Thank you. And thank you for having the dogs and me today."

"Oh, honey, you're as good as family now. You're welcome any time. Let me see this ring." Barbara held Catherine's hand. "It's beautiful. You did a good job, Joe." She released Catherine's hand and motioned her to follow. "Let's introduce you to the significant others of the family and enjoy the day."

Cat slid her hand in Josef's, and he gently squeezed it.

"Did you bring your suits? The water feels great," Adam yelled from the lake, standing next to a raft, where a very pregnant Maureen lay.

"That's Adam and Maureen," he whispered in her ear and then

bellowed, "I have mine, but Cat didn't pack one." This gained Tiffany's attention as she ran to join them. "Tiff, this is Catherine—Catherine, Tiffany."

"I've got a bikini that would look cute on you. You can borrow it."

"Thanks, but I'm not ready to go swimming right now."

"Just let me know when you want it."

John approached, sliding his arm around Tiff's waist. "Hey, Cat, good to see you," he said, holding out his hand which she took.

"Nice to see you, too, John."

"You've met Tiffany, my girlfriend. David and Marlene are out on the paddleboat." John nodded to the lake in the direction of the boat.

They stepped onto the patio by the shoreline, and his father, Walter, greeted him with a man's hug. "Happy Fourth, Dad. You remember Catherine," Josef said.

"Yes. Catherine, my condolences to you and your family."

"Thank you, Walter."

Everyone sat, and Josef said, "We applied for our marriage license on Monday, and the license should be ready in a week. So, anytime next weekend or after."

"Joe, we can't plan a wedding in two weeks," his mother interjected.

"We're getting married by the Justice of the Peace." He delivered a gentle squeeze to Cat's hand.

"Why not at the church?" his mother asked, disappointed.

"Because Father Tim won't allow it."

"What?" his mother exclaimed. "I'm going to give him a call. Our family has been going to that church for centuries and has given—"

"Mom." Josef touched her arm. "Stop. Father Tim won't change his mind. He has his own ulterior motive." Cat sidled up next to him, and he wrapped his arm her. "Elaine's will states the trust fund goes to St. Michael's if Cat doesn't get married. Father's out to get the money, and the only way he can control that is by not letting us get married in the church."

"That's so wrong," Tiff piped in. "He can't do that."

"Yes, he can," Cat chimed in. "It's his right as head of the church."

"How does your mother feel about all this?" his mother asked Cat.

"She's excited to think I might find someone and get married. But my family doesn't know yet about the engagement. I can't tell them over the phone. I plan on telling them when I return to the cities."

"Well, I can tell you this. She's not going to like it either."

A warm breeze blew, and leaves rustled, making their own music as a wind chime would. The humidity in the air grew heavier, and Josef wiped at his brow.

"Mom, let us take care of it. Cat and I haven't even discussed the wedding yet. We're in the waiting process for the license. I'm going to look into the JP after the holiday week, and we'll go from there."

"Catherine, you tell your mother to call me after you inform them of the good news."

"I will. If you'll excuse me, I should probably get the dogs out of the house. Josef, can you help me?"

He stood and followed Cat into the yard and stepped beside her. "Everything okay? Are you mad?"

"No. Why would I be mad?"

"I don't know. You just seem—"

"I have a lot on my mind. Things are happening so fast, and your mom is right about the wedding."

"What do ya mean she's right?" He opened the lower level patio door and let Cat in first.

"My mom's not going to be happy if we don't have a wedding. We'll need to plan something small with the judge."

Josef closed the door. "If you and your mother want to plan something I'm fine with that. But we'll need to set a date then."

"Fine. Can we talk about it later? Let's enjoy the day. I need the dogs' leashes."

She stepped toward the stairs, and he snatched her hand. "They don't need their leashes." He held of both hands, "Let them run and play in the lake."

"I … fine, but if something happens …"

"Nothing's going to happen." He released her hands and strolled behind the bar. "What do ya want to drink?"

"I'll take a beer. Maybe it will help me relax."

Josef pulled two beers from the fridge and handed her one. The dogs thundered down the stairs. "So what happened that makes you so protective of the dogs?"

"I've lost dogs to car accidents, to them running away. I've witnessed so much since becoming a vet. I … I just don't want anything to happen to my own pets or anyone else's."

"I understand, Cat, but you also need to let them be dogs. Let them run and play. Let them jump and swim in the lake. They'll be okay here. The farm is new to them, and I understand and respect your decision to keep them on chains." He kissed her. "Let's go out and rejoin the family." At the patio door, he let the dogs run through first. She accepted the hand he offered as they crossed the lawn.

They sat on the patio, with the conversation focusing on what Cat did for a living, her family and briefly about her rescue mission for the horses and other animals. They sat by the lake for over an hour talking while the afternoon sun and humidity warmed Josef. "I'm hot." He eyed Cat. "Want to take a dip in the lake?"

Cat turned to Tiffany. "Do you mind if I borrow that bikini now? I'm hot too, and the lake would probably feel really good."

"Sure." Tiffany and Cat disappeared into the house.

A short time later, Cat walked out wearing a hot pink bikini. Reminded of the other night, with so much flesh exposed, Josef's body reacted. His heart revved. He pushed the feeling aside, along with a desire to have her in his bed again.

Everyone commented about how good she looked in the suit, from the color to the fit. Even his brothers had something to say.

"You look good in Tiff's suit. Are you ready?" Josef asked, holding out a hand for her, which she accepted.

"Let's go. I need to cool down."

"Me, too. My mind is being molesting by visions of you wearing that bikini," Josef said as he wiggled his brows at her.

They jumped together and went beneath the lake's surface. When they came up, the dogs followed, jumping behind them. They all swam to shallower waters. They played with the dogs for a short time and grabbed a large floating raft for two.

Josef kicked them to deeper waters and carefully hoisted himself onto the raft. "The family likes you. I think the girls like having a new addition to the family."

"They're all very nice. I like them, too." With a long pause, she asked, "When is Maureen due?"

"Next month. This heat's been hard on her, so she's spending a lot of time here." Lying on their stomachs with arms stretched out beside their heads, hands rested in the water as they looked ahead. Boats passed by, and their wakes gently rocked the raft.

"Um, after the other night—" Cat started with a serious tone that caught his attention.

He faced her as she continued to face forward. "It wasn't that bad, was it?" he asked.

"Ah, no. That's not the direction I was going. We're getting married and that fulfills the will, but since the other night I've been wondering. The will mentioned children ... and I was wondering ...even more so since seeing Maureen pregnant—" She met his gaze when he interrupted.

"I don't want kids now. Not right away." He was glad she brought up the subject. Letting her lead the way in this marriage-to-be was working out well.

"Good. Because neither do I. But—"

"But what? If we agree, there shouldn't be a *'but'* in there." Resting on one arm, he didn't care for the direction the conversation was going.

"If you'd let me finish." Her voice came out upset and serious.

"Sorry."

"We need to face the fact that we didn't use protection, and I could be ..." She held his eyes. Another boat passed, rocking them with more force.

Speechless, his arm collapsed beneath him. He'd been wrapped up in the moment and forgot to wrap *it* up. A kid would only complicate things with a divorce. "When will you know?"

"In a week."

She didn't sound happy. In fact, she sounded afraid. He'd better say the right thing. Or early fireworks would blow up in his face and in front of the family. *Shit!*

"We'll just wait and see what happens. If you are, well then we'll start our family earlier than planned." He took her hand beneath the water's surface and stroked her fingers. "It'll be all right."

Silence was good and bad at this moment. Josef continued to hold her hand, unable to decipher her feelings about the possibility of a family. Unable to decipher his own. She seemed concerned, yet okay with it, too. He remained quiet, not wanting to say the wrong thing or ask too many questions without knowing what was going on inside her head.

Their peace and quiet came to an end when someone yelled, "You might want to come a little closer to shore before we have to send out a rescue boat."

Josef sat up and looked around in surprise. Shore was a half mile away. "Ah, shit. I guess I'd better get kicking." He scooted down the raft.

They laughed as his legs hung over the back and kicked. Cat used her hands to keep them in the right direction. The dogs jumped into the lake as they neared shore.

"We make a good team." Not getting a verbal response, but a vague smile, he knew the potential pregnancy weighed heavily on her mind. It would be on his mind, too. "Hey, get down," he said to the dogs as they tried to get on the raft. "Down."

Cat slid into the water and greeted the dogs while he pulled the raft onto shore. She joined the women lying in the sun, except Maureen who was in the shade on the patio. Josef joined the rest of the family.

It pleased him to see her relax with the dogs being off their leashes, letting them run and enjoy the lake. Even Fritz was in the water having fun. Every now and then, Josef would peer in her direction, and a funny feeling settled in his gut. Love was taking over the vacancy in his heart.

* * * *

Cat woke to a touch on her shoulder and heard Josef's voice.

"Cat, time to get ready for dinner."

Her eyes, mere slits, adjusted to the brightness. He sat next to her.

"You okay?"

"Just a little …" She didn't finish because she didn't want to think of the possibility.

"You've had a lot going on. Guess your body needed the rest. It doesn't mean anything. It's too soon."

"I know." She wiped her brow free of sweat. "But why didn't you wake me so I could help in the kitchen?"

"Mom wouldn't have let you help if you tried. You're a guest, but when we're married that will be a different story."

"Good. I guess I should get changed." She stood. Light headed, she reached out and held on to Josef's shoulder. "Shit."

"I don't think you've drank enough fluids. This warm weather has gotten the better of you."

"Yeah, whatever." She felt bad for saying it because he was only trying to make her feel more at ease about the possibility of being pregnant. "I'm going to change."

* * * *

She managed to keep her composure during dinner, but every time she saw Maureen's swollen belly she wanted to cry. This was getting the better of her, and she didn't like it.

The table cleared of dishes, Josef pulled her into a bedroom. "Do you want to leave? It's okay if ya do. I really don't mind."

"I'd like that if you're sure it's okay." Her head wasn't in the right place to have fun for the holiday celebration.

They returned to the kitchen, and Cat stayed at Josef's side.

"Mom, we're going to leave. Cat's tired, and we have a lot to talk about."

"Are you feeling well, dear?" Barbara stepped from the sink, wiping her hands dry on the floral apron.

"I'll be fine. I think I just need to get some sleep."

"You're not—"

"Mom!"

Catherine burst into tears.

"We need to leave." Josef gathered her in his arms.

"I—"

"Mom, I love you, but let it go. I'll call you."

Catherine let him guide her to the truck and round up the dogs while she waited and cried in the pickup. She was messed up. The universe was working against her. She wanted the chaos to end.

Josef got in and headed home. "Sorry about my mom. I didn't think she'd say anything like that."

"It's ... o ... kay. How ... were ... you ... to know?" She struggled

91

to talk through the tears and sniffles. They rode in silence until they neared the Oak City exit.

"The air conditioning will feel nice as well as a shower after being in the lake."

She nodded while wiping her nose.

"The bed will feel good, too. No fireworks tonight. I want to be there to comfort you."

She laughed. "Comfort me, my ass."

"You're not nice." There was hurt in his voice.

"I'm sorry."

"Give me some credit, Cat." He was serious.

"Okay. I'm sorry. Really."

"Really?"

"Yes."

"Can I get a kiss?"

She leaned into him and quickly kissed his lips. Nothing further than a kiss could happen between them. Nothing.

Chapter Thirteen

Catherine stepped from Josef's bedroom and paused; the house was quiet. After feeding her dogs, she wandered to her Aunt Elaine's to feed the kittens. Josef was at work in the field. Last night he held her under the spray of warm water in the shower while she cried. The possibility of being pregnant weighed on her mind then as it did now. He reminded her why they were getting married, that a baby wouldn't change his mind. He'd told her he wasn't going anywhere and when they crawled under the covers, he held her close and caressed her hair until she fell asleep.

The warm sticky morning air foretold of a storm like the one brewing in her life. She went into the farmhouse. Silence. A reminder of why she was staying at Josef's.

Damned water. Catherine cursed quietly while filling the bowls with kitten food. It all started with a pipe bursting. She walked down the cement stairs and strolled across the yard to the barn. *I would've been just fine without the water, but no, the refrigerator had to take a shit, too.* A gentle breeze blew across her shoulders, and goose bumps covered her arms. She shivered.

At the barn door, she balanced the food bowl on top of the water bowl, careful not to spill when she pulled on the rusty handle. The kittens mewed, running to her feet at her entrance. Mindful of where she stepped, she stopped a few steps into the barn and placed the bowls on the floor.

She sat on a nearby hay bale. This would be the end of her involvement with the kittens. They were farm cats and would remain just that—farm cats. They were needed in the barn to kill mice. A kitten jumped and rubbed against her thigh.

"Hey, Fluffy." She petted the kitten from head to tail. "You and your siblings are getting big." The cat's motor ran loudly with a vibration Catherine couldn't miss. "You like being loved, huh?"

Love. Did Josef love her? Or was this all for what they wanted? What her aunt didn't give them. Did her aunt do this on purpose? How could she have known? Josef had a good point when they talked about marriage at first. "Why, Aunt Elaine? Why?"

"It will all work out," a woman's voice whispered on the wind.

Another subtle breeze caressed her shoulders, and Catherine jumped. She twisted, looking for who spoke. No one was there but the kittens. "What will all work out?"

No answer.

"I'm hearing things."

"Meeooow."

"I'll be fine, Fluffy. But it's time for me to go." One last pet and she stood. "I'll be back later." She gathered the empty bowls and exited the barn.

The dogs played in Josef's front yard, but he wasn't in sight. *Time to go shopping.* She went inside, grabbed her keys and purse and left for town.

Clouds moved in from the west. A little rain would help alleviate some of the heat and humidity. The windows up and the air conditioning blowing a cool breeze, she turned up the country song on the radio. She pulled into the Walmart parking lot fifteen minutes later.

Fresh baked bread wafted in her direction as she entered the store. Her stomach grumbled in protest. You couldn't miss the Subway sign. She went to the counter and ordered. Sub in hand, she walked with determined steps to the pharmaceutical department.

Her eyes scanned the aisles for what she wanted and to make sure she didn't see anyone who would recognize her. Her heart beat military style—double time, with the possibility of being pregnant or seen purchasing a pregnancy test.

Catherine picked up the pregnancy test and flipped the box to read the back. *Five days. I can't wait that long.*

Several boxes later, she decided on one and approached the

pharmacy to pay.

"Shit," she said silently through quick breaths.

Jackson stood behind the counter in a white lab coat. She mumbled a quick prayer he wouldn't see her and made a u-turn for the front of the store. The self-checkout lane offered some privacy and a fast escape.

In her truck she took a deep breath to help relax. Her hands shook. Another calming breath and she told herself, "He didn't see me. It'll be okay."

She turned the key, and the air-conditioning blew cool air while she sat and ate in the confines of her vehicle. Between bites she read the instructions for the pregnancy test. All of the tests stated to take after a missed menstrual cycle. Not before. She purchased the box containing two tests rather than one. This allowed her to take one now and see the result without waiting a week. Then if necessary, she'd use the other test later. Hungry for a sugary treat, she knew right where to go.

The bell clanged above her head as the door opened and closed. "Hey, Harvey! How are you?"

The old man sat behind the register listening to a weather radio squawk.

"We could have some bad weather coming our way. Make sure you get home and stay home. Have the TV on."

"Is that what they're saying?" She perused the candy selection.

"Storms are moving in from the west, and wall clouds have been spotted but no tornadoes." He stood and gave her amused stare. "You need more of them baked beans?" He chuckled at his own humor, she suspected.

She glanced at his smiling face. Gentle eyes crinkled at the corners, and his scrunched nose pushed his glasses. "You know me." A box of Boston Baked Beans rattled, and she set a cellophane tube full of Sixlets, a box of Chiclets and the box of beans on the counter. "This should do me."

"That'll be a dollar-sixty."

She handed the money to Harvey. "Thanks."

He took hold of her left hand and whistled. "This is new. He's a lucky man."

She slowly removed her hand. "Thank you. Have a good night,

Harvey."

"You, too. Remember to stay safe in this storm."

"I will," she said, exiting the store.

The air had cooled and the clouds changed from gray to a dark gray with the promise of rain. In her truck, she opened the windows and then the small package of Sixlets, pouring a mouthful. Her tongue moved them from cheek to cheek before she crunched through the candy coating. Her eyes closed as the chocolate melted, and her head tipped back at the delicious taste. Eyes opened, she poured in another mouthful. Rain sputtered the front glass, and she put the windows up.

The plastic bag containing the pregnancy test sat on the seat. She stuffed the bag into the bottom of her purse. Josef didn't need to know. Right now it was strictly a need-to-know situation. She'd get to the farm, go to the bathroom and take the test. It was as simple as that.

* * * *

Josef stepped from the barn and spotted Cat's pickup. The moment of relief didn't last long. The heavy rain had passed, but the dark gray skies had taken on an ominous green tint. In the distance a dark wall cloud approached, like an ancient enemy war line. He scanned the fast looming cloud and spotted the formation. Tornado! The winds picked up, blowing dust from the dirt road around. Trees began to twist and bow under the force of extreme winds.

"Blondie! Where are you, girl?" He hollered for the yellow Lab while running to the front yard. "There you are. Good girl."

Hail the size of a quarter fell from the quickly darkening sky. He unchained Cat's three dogs and with a raised voice yelled while motioning with his arm, "Let's go. Inside. Now!" He ran for the front porch door, holding it open as they darted through.

The front door secured, he yelled with quickened breaths. "Cat? Cat, we got to get to the basement. Now!" He ran down the hall to close the back door. Golf ball sized hail pounded the ground, coming thick and hard from the dark green-grey sky. His heart pounded like the hail outside. He searched for Cat. His stomach contracted into a tight ball. Where was she?

"Cat? Come on, we need to get to the basement—now," he

exclaimed opening the door beneath the stairs leading to the crawl space. His pulse roared in his ears. "Cat," he screamed, questioning her whereabouts.

"I'm in the bathroom. Give me a minute."

"We don't have a minute. I've got the dogs." He ran toward her voice. She was in the bathroom off the kitchen. "A tornado's headed our way."

"Shit," she exclaimed, swinging the door with more force than needed as it banged into the wall. The winds turned into a menacing roar.

"This way." He pulled her by the hand. He turned the light on in the small area beneath the first level. With her fear of basements, he hoped she wouldn't hesitate to go in.

"Are you okay?" He secured the thick door, stooped while going down the four steps. The house wasn't designed with a basement, but he had worked with the builder to get the small area built. A tornado shelter in Minnesota was a must-have. He kept a few comfort items, a radio and flashlights stored in the room.

"Fine."

"So is it all basements or just Elaine's that you're afraid of?" He wiped his sweaty palms on his pant legs and turned on the radio.

"Most, but not all of them."

His attention turned from comforting Cat to hoping the tornado would pass them by.

"We have reports of a tornado on the ground," the weatherman stated. "If you are in the Oak City area, you should already be in a sheltered area."

The four dogs curled up together on the floor in the farthest corner, their soft whines and shivering bodies an indication they knew trouble wasn't far away.

Josef's heart rate returned to a semi-normal state with everyone safe. He rolled out a foam bed, shook open a blanket and leaned two pillows against the wall. "Hope this is okay."

"I'll be fine." She crawled onto the bed and leaned against the wall. "You're well prepared."

"In this state you should be prepared for any event. So … what's with you and basements?" Having done all he could to keep them safe despite the sound of furious winds, he picked up his earlier question about her fear.

"I told you. I don't like narrow stairwells. And old basements really creep me out."

"That's all? There has to be more." The windows and door rattled above them. They both fell silent.

Cat scooted closer to him, and he pulled her shaking body into him. He placed the blanket over their legs.

"When I was ten, I found my grandfather," she whispered, struggling for words.

"What do you mean *found*?"

"He was slumped over at the bottom of the stairs. I tried to wake him up, but he just wouldn't wake up," she cried.

Josef didn't have anything to wipe away her tears. His heart grew heavy with grief for her. "Which grandfather?"

She answered between sniffles. "My dad's father. We were at my grandparent's home. He had a heart attack."

"I don't understand how ... why you don't like basements?"

"I'm afraid of being alone ... like he was. In a dark creepy place."

Josef held her tighter and felt bad for the way he made fun of her for never going downstairs at Elaine's. He could never imagine what it would be like to find someone dead when you're ten years old. "I'm sorry, Catherine, for teasing you and for you being the one to find him."

"It's okay. You didn't know. Their house wasn't as old as Elaine's farm, but the basement was dark. The stairwell was very steep with a low ceiling as you neared the bottom."

Josef liked how she fit into him and was glad she didn't move. There was silence between them once more as the wind howled and windows rattled.

They both jumped when glass shattered somewhere above, followed by heavy thuds.

"I don't like the sound of things." He caressed her arm to comfort them both.

"Me either." She snuggled deeper into him.

A tornado was in the vicinity. How much devastation would it make? How many lives would be lost? Would they be okay?

In spite of the danger above them, the lantern light caught the diamond's sparkled on her left hand. He smiled at the thought of being able to hold her every night in his arms. Could the love they lost be found?

Cat's brown eyes met his. Yup, his heart found the love, and he wouldn't let go. He kissed the top of her head and whispered, "I love you."

Silence.

Did she hear him? Could she not say anything? Was she unsure how to respond?

As much as he fought his feelings for her, he knew all along it would be difficult *not* to fall in love again. He had never really stopped loving her. It was her who didn't love him. This was why he had never pushed to keep a relationship going in the past, but instead focused on getting the farmland back.

Not just Cat's silence—silence above them.

"It's awfully quiet. Do you think the storm's passed?" she asked, sitting up out of his embrace.

"You stay here while I take a look." He crawled to the stairs, approached the door and listened. "It's over." He rejoined Cat and picked up the pillows and blanket. "Pretty certain a tornado touched down though."

Chapter Fourteen

Josef's massive arms spread out to the sides blocking the doorway, and she stopped. Shattered glass lay strewn across the wood floor. Night's darkness followed in the wake of the destruction. A measurable size of wood replaced his dining room table. The beam of light from his flashlight scanned the area.

"Let me walk around before you move." He lowered his arms. "I want to make sure it's safe."

"Okay." Things appeared okay. The house still stood. Just broken windows.

He disappeared for several minutes. "My room's okay." He passed her, headed in the direction of the kitchen before returning. "Inside we're okay except for these front windows. Appears we've acquired some building materials." He chuckled, digging through a drawer in the china cabinet.

She smiled and giggled a little. Cat missed his humor. And until recently missed his touch. Could he ever love her again? She'd hurt him. Could this marriage survive based only on the convenience without a love for each other? Her heart, mind, body and soul fell in love with Josef all over again. He had shown compassion on more than one occasion in the last few weeks, leading her to believe love could be found between them again.

The dogs stood on the stairs behind her and bolted through the front door to get outside.

"Fuzzy, Darby—"

"They'll be fine. They need to go to the bathroom." He turned on a flashlight and handed it to her. "Careful."

The movie *Jurassic Park* came to mind as she pointed the flashlight out into the darkness. Big oak tree branches loomed at her when illuminated by the light beam. Debris from the trees added to building pieces littered the yard. Her truck appeared to be intact except for the busted-out windows.

"How's it look over there?" she hollered to Josef, who checked the garage.

"The one door's pushed against the back of my truck. Can't see if there's any damage." He walked to the shed where that big green hunk of machinery was parked.

She carefully made her way to join him and heard a phone ring. Not her ring tone, she held her light up and Josef pulled his phone from his front pocket.

"Hello?—Yeah, we're fine.—Cat's still here.—How 'bout you?—Good.—No. The front windows are shattered, and my truck may need some work.—Shit, I didn't even think about that.—Sounds good, I will." He shoved the phone back in his pocket.

"Who was that?"

"Wayne. He's okay. The tornado missed them. We need to go check Elaine's."

They stepped carefully around branches, pieces of wood planks, twisted pieces of metal and stalks of corn. It was a tossed debris salad without dressing. They reached the end of his driveway, lifted their flashlights and together in flat unison said, "Shit."

Josef gripped her fingertips. "Let's go get a better look."

She couldn't move. Like an anvil, her stomach dropped and landed hard, leaving her at the bottom of the hole it created in the ground. She didn't need a better look to know that it was gone. All gone. Catherine fell to her knees. Gravel bit into her exposed flesh. The flashlight fell to the ground and illuminated the culvert. She covered her face and sobbed.

"Cat, we can rebuild. I'm sure the base of the barn is still there." He knelt beside her. His head tipped to look at her. "We can put up new fencing. Hell," he lifted her chin up, "we can build you and the horses a brand new barn the way you want it."

"I can't go." Tears streamed down her cheeks. She wiped them away. "Not now."

"Okay." He stood. "I won't be gone long. Nothing we can do anyway."

"The kittens! I forgot about them." Tears flowed as she covered her face. "What happened to them?"

"What kittens?"

"There were six kittens in the barn." She swiped her face. "I was feeding them. Oh, you need to let me know."

"I'll be back." He delivered a gentle kiss on her lips. "We'll rebuild for you and the horses. It'll be okay. *We* can get through this."

Josef crossed the road into darkness, a flashlight his beacon.

Two wet noses nuzzled each of Cat's arms. "Fuzzy. Fritz." She patted each of them and rubbed their back ends. "Where's Darby?" She picked up the flashlight and moved the light beam around the yard.

"Rrruff," Fuzzy responded and bounded for the front yard.

The two Labs played with each other. Maybe there was more than one love relationship happening on the farm. She meandered to the front porch with Fritz following her. Catherine gathered the sticks and branches littering the porch floor and made a pile. She righted the overturned bench, switched off the flashlight and sat in the darkness. Waiting.

They could rebuild. Rebuild the barn. Rebuild their trust. Rebuild their love. She had fallen in love with him all over again. She believed he had, too. He had said the three little words earlier.

Josef's beacon in the night shone her way, and the silence was broken by his quiet voice. "All gone—mess.—Yes—married. I want that land back.—She doesn't know.—I've got to go. I can't see her. Just be here in the morning to help."

The conversation cut in and out at first but became clearer as he neared his farm ... and her. He didn't want to marry her to help her, but for his own reasons. She knew he wanted to continue farming Elaine's land and the marriage would allow that to happen, but she didn't know he actually *wanted* the land. Anger overflowed her veins. She'd be damned if she'd marry him now.

So much for love and trust.

Cat grabbed the flashlight, entered the house and went upstairs. She turned the flashlight on and threw clothing into her bag.

Josef stood in the bedroom doorway. "What are ya doing?"

"What does it look like?"

"Packing. But why?" Hunched shoulders and hands out to his side, he clearly had no idea what was going on.

"I'm leaving. It's over." She pinched the engagement ring, and with a slight tug, slid it from her finger and threw it on the counter. "There will be no wedding."

He didn't go after the ring that fell somewhere to the floor.

She pushed passed him, only to be stopped by his large hands. "Don't say that. Why not?"

"You said it yourself, you *want that* land." A deluge of rage made her voice rise and crack. "I don't know what the hell you were talking about or to whom …" Her fingers curled into tight fists. "… but you can call them back and let them know the wedding is off, and you won't be getting *that* land back." She wiggled. "Let me go."

"*That* land should be back in my family."

"I don't know what the hell you're talking about. And I don't give a damned. Let me go." She squirmed and freed herself from his hold.

She stomped down the stairs, out the door and to her truck. Damn! Before putting the dogs in the truck the broken glass would need to be cleaned out. In front of her, a light from behind illuminated a path. Josef. *Damn him.*

"What do you think you're doing?" She tossed her bag in the back end and snatched the hand broom she kept for use at the barn. "I can clean up my own mess. You have your own to clean."

"I can help if I want," his tone soft and caring.

Did he think she would change her mind if he was sweet and loving? Hell no! It only added fuel to the fire.

"Fine. Suit yourself." Her hand shook as she swept the glass. Finished, she moved to the other side. "I'll finish here." Her jaw clenched.

"Your truck took a beating by the debris being thrown around. You'll want to call your insurance agent."

She ignored him and yanked a blanket from behind the rear seat and spread it across the seat for the dogs' protection. Who knew what remained stuck in the cushions.

With a tight grip on the flashlight, she stomped through the front yard to find and gather the dog chains.

"Cat, don't go. Let's talk."

"There is *nothing* for us to talk about. It's over, Josef." She ripped a chain anchor out of the dirt. "Over." Chains in hand, she marched to the rear of the pickup.

"What if you're—?"

"You don't need to worry about it. We had sex once. Chances of me being pregnant are slim." Who the hell was she kidding? Her stomach revolted at the comment. Tossing the chains in the back, she hollered out, "Let's go, boys."

The four dogs nimbly came. Blondie lay by Josef's leg.

"Careful getting in," she told the dogs as she held the blanket in place.

Bloody paw prints appeared on the blanket.

The festering fury boiled over.

"I never should've listened to you," she turned and screamed at Josef. "Do you see this?" she asked, pointing to the blanket. "Because you let them run out of the house, their feet are all cut up. Damn it, Josef." She spun on her heals and pulled her small emergency vet box from the back.

"I'm sorry, Cat."

She squatted in front of Blondie and picked up one paw at a time, inspecting for injury. "Let's get her in the house." She closed the door, containing her dogs inside the truck. "You need to keep her inside until this mess is cleaned up. Pick her up and bring her inside."

"Cat, I'm sorry. I didn't—"

"No, you didn't think. Don't apologize. I'll need you to hold a flashlight. Let's go to the kitchen."

"Anything. I'll do anything for you."

"Put her on the kitchen island. Good. Now hold the light on her paws while I work on them." Cat didn't have the full means to treat the dogs, but what she could do now would be better than nothing.

She poured water on the paw to clean away the dirt and any loose particles. Using tweezers, she pulled the pieces of glass from the pads of

Blondie's foot, depositing the shards in a bowl. When she felt she had all the debris removed, she poured water over the paw, applied antibiotic ointment and wrapped the entire foot up the leg in gauze.

"You're good. Thank you." He spoke the humbling words softly.

"Make sure she sees her regular vet tomorrow." She worked on the next paw.

"I will. Please don't leave, Cat." The flashlight moved from Blondie's paw to her.

"Damn it, Josef. Keep the light on her paw. I'm working."

The beam of light shone on the dog's paw. For the remainder of the cleaning procedure, Josef kept his mouth shut. Catherine finished the fourth paw and cleaned her utensils at the sink. Padded paws walked out the room while boots moved closer to her. His warmth permeated her back.

Don't turn around. Don't listen to him. Don't trust him.

"I'm sorry, Cat. Don't go." His breath tickled her neck. Her stomach fluttered.

She closed her eyes, took a deep breath, opened her eyes, placed the last item in her box and snapped the locks.

His arms slid around her sides, and his hands rested on the counter—trapping her. His chest hammered against her back. She swung her arm, knocking his from the ledge.

With a firm voice she stated, "I'm done here," and walked with defiance out the front door.

As she approached her truck and got behind the wheel, he ran toward her, yelling, "Cat, don't go. I love you."

"Goodbye, Josef," were her final words as she sped out of the drive.

Chapter Fifteen

A cat pounced on Catherine's chest Friday morning, instantly waking her. "I'm awake." Little Buddy purred and rubbed her soft furry head on Catherine's chin. "I know. You're happy to have me home." But was *she* happy to be home? As angry as she was, she missed the farm.

Tossing the covers to the side, she sat on the edge of the bed for a moment. The dogs' ears perked, and their heads popped up. "Okay, everyone. Breakfast time."

With the animals fed, it was her turn to eat. No milk in the house, or much of anything else, she poured cranberry pomegranate juice over her granola cereal. She crunched through breakfast and decided to confront her mother today about the will. She thought about Josef. The marriage. The land. Their love.

"Oh, hell no!" Her hands slammed on the table. "I do *not* love him."

Three dog heads lifted from their food bowls. With heads tipped to the side, they looked at her as though they had done something wrong. The dogs stuffed their faces back into bowls, probably thinking their human was crazy and talking to herself.

What was she thinking? Love? She couldn't love Josef. Love was a powerful word. After last night, love no longer existed. He deceived her.

The last bite of cereal disappeared, and she put the dogs outside. Looking out the patio door she glanced around at the surroundings. Rows of townhomes lined up. Backed up to one another. No privacy. She had a small grass area the builder association called a yard, with tall white maintenance free privacy fencing to separate her patio from the neighboring patios. Trees and shrubs sparsely spread out for shade and

106

ambiance.

She missed the farm's wide-open space and turned from the view. Closing her eyes, she leaned against the wall, envisioning the big mature oak tree in the center of Aunt Elaine's circle drive and the wide open spaces between the buildings and barn. It was all gone now. Everything destroyed by the tornado. The tornado destroyed dreams of a new home for her horses. Yet she could still have it if she wanted. Two years and she could build her dream on the old farmland.

Time to save money and read the fine print of the contract Elaine had with Josef. Her contract. She would start right away building a small house and barn. And make her own memories.

Several messages popped up when she turned on her cell phone. Her mother wanted to know how things were going. Catherine would let her know soon enough. Four from Josef asking her to come back so they could talk. The next time they talked, construction would begin on her land.

* * * *

"Mom?" Catherine sung out, entering her childhood home. "Are you here?"

"Catherine," Margaret exclaimed, walking from the kitchen wearing her grapevine covered apron with the statement, *Cooking with wine is like cooking with chocolate. Sometimes you have to try a sample.*

Catherine grinned at the wine apron. The wording always made her smirk.

"When did you get home?" Her mom embraced her. "We were worried about you and Josef when the weather turned nasty." Concern shone on her mom's face as she released the hold. "Is everything okay?"

"No. We need to talk."

"Sounds serious. Is the kitchen okay? I'm making sauce for tonight."

"Fine." She followed. "It smells delicious as always."

"I'm so lucky your grandmother took the time and had the patience to teach me the family recipe. Otherwise, I don't know what your father would've done. He-a needs-a his-a authentic –a Italian-a sauce-a." Catherine chuckled at her mom's attempt at an Italian dialect. "Yous-a

107

laugh. That's-a good."

"Enough, Mom." She sat at the marbled kitchen ledge on a black iron high-backed chair. "How involved were you in the writing of Aunt Elaine's will?"

"Catherine." Her mom stood at the stove and stirred the tomato sauce.

"I'm serious. I want to know."

Margaret stepped to the plastic cutting board and worked on an onion. She wasn't answering.

"Mom?" Her firm voice gained no response.

Her mom sliced the onion and chopped the slices into small pieces.

"So you did have something to do with it?" Her voice hitched several octaves. Catherine let her mom finish with the onion, stirring it into the sauce mix, before speaking. "I want to know. I need to know. Damn it, I have a right to know."

"Catherine!" Margaret said with a firm voice.

She had overstepped her vocal boundary as a daughter.

Catherine took a moment to compose herself. "Were you and Aunt Elaine hoping Josef and I would get married? Do you have money invested in the trust fund?"

"What would make you even think such a thing?" Her mom turned from the stove, returned to the cutting board and cut fresh herbs. Margaret wouldn't look at her.

"It doesn't answer my question, but then again maybe it does."

Silence filled the spacious kitchen. Her mom's non-answers were answers enough.

"What is the story behind the farm? Josef said something about the land belonging to his family. Do you know what he's talking about?"

"Your great-grandfather and Josef's great-grandfather were playing in a poker game one night. Josef's great-grandfather bet some of his farmland."

"Oh my God. It's true then." She leaned forward with an elbow resting on the counter while the fingers on her other hand twisted a section of hair as her mother continued.

"No. It rightfully belonged to *your* great-grandfather and so on down the line. It does not belong to Josef or his family. Josef's great-grandfather owned the land Josef lives and farms on now. Your great-grandfather built the farmhouse, where it sits today, to flaunt his winning in front of Josef's great-grandfather."

Her mom stepped from the stove, approached the marble counter where Catherine sat, reached out and held her hand. "I did talk at great length with Elaine about her wishes and the will. Yes, it was her hope you and Josef would see things through and get married."

"That's why she gave us the opposite of what she knew we wanted." Catherine sat back, contemplating the information. She wasn't mad. She couldn't be mad. It was her aunt's will. Catherine didn't have to do anything if she didn't want to.

"Yes. She also hoped for the marriage because then the land would become Josef's and be back in his family. She knew how much the land meant to him, but I don't think she was aware he knew the history of the land."

"Why the marriage trust fund though?" The hair wound around her finger as her mom tended to the pot on the stove.

"I have nothing to do with the trust fund monies. Elaine felt it would work as an incentive."

"Where did she get the money? Before she … We were talking about the house and all the work she had done. She mentioned not having to take out a loan and using the money made from leasing the land to Josef. How could she afford that large amount?"

"I don't know. She was smart with her finances."

"But why put a time restraint on it then?"

"Elaine knew if she didn't put a time frame on the marriage request, then it might never happen. She wanted the money to go someplace where it would be put to good use. She believed in you and Four Hooves and Paws. She thought the money could help you."

Quiet filled the room. Catherine's mind twirled like a spinning top, out of control with the new information. But did it change anything? No, because Josef's marriage proposal was based on what he wanted. He didn't care about her. Or did he?

"What happened with Josef?" Her mother broke the silence and her thoughts.

"Josef proposed, I said yes, we went to his parents for the holiday, the tornado came and destroyed everything. I broke off the engagement and came home."

"What?" Margaret exclaimed. She dashed to the counter and yanked Catherine's left hand from her hair twisting. "Josef—you—engaged?"

"Not any longer." She reclaimed her hand and resumed twisting. "I have no reason to marry him. Aunt Elaine's farm is gone. The tornado destroyed everything. I overheard a phone conversation and that's when I found out he wanted to marry me only because of the land."

"I think you need to answer the question of why *you* said yes, Catherine." Her mom took on that motherly consoling tone and faced Catherine with questioning eyes.

Before she could answer her mother, her phone rang. Josef.

Chapter Sixteen

Josef sat on his bed, staring at the ring on his pointer finger. The silver shone, and the diamond sparkled rainbows around the room. Last night sleep came in spurts as he struggled with worry for Cat. Everything happened between them in such a short amount of time. He had to get the ring back on her finger.

Blondie barked, followed by a knock at the door. "Hey, Joe, you in there?"

"I'm here, Wayne." He sauntered into the dining room. "Just a minute." He pulled the small black velvet box from the china hutch drawer and placed the solitaire diamond ring inside.

"Where's Cat?"

"She heard me talking to ya last night and left." He tossed the box in the drawer and slammed it shut with a clenched jaw. "She won't answer my calls or respond to my messages."

"She broke things off?"

"Yes, but I'm not giving up." The situation between him and Cat was too fresh for him to talk, friend or no friend. "Help me get this shit out of here." Josef walked into the living room and waited for Wayne to help him lift the wood off what was once his dining room table. "Looks like a chunk of Elaine's barn. Couldn't tell in the dark last night."

"I saw the damage."

"Damage? It's a total loss. Cat has nowhere to move the horses now." His heart wrung with pity.

"What about you? How are you handling all of this? You lost the house and barn, and the sheds look damaged, and you and Cat aren't getting married."

"I'm fine and don't need the reminder, thank you." The ice in his voice could chill the beer he'd drink later. He grabbed an end of the wood section. "Now help me lift this and get it outside."

They carried the section of barn to the porch and threw it into the front lawn.

"You want some help boarding the windows."

"Nah. I'm going to use the plastic winter window stuff to cover them. Let's go to Elaine's. I need to see things in the daylight."

Dale's police cruiser sat at the end of Elaine's driveway, and he stood surveying the damage.

"Hey, Dale," Josef said, approaching the front yard. "Can we come take a look?"

"Watch where you're walking. I called the city for the cleanup crew. They'll be out later today."

"Who else got hit?" Josef asked.

"Olson's and Plemel's but not to this extent. They have damage that appears to be repairable. Crops have been lost, but no loss in lives. Hey," Dale glanced around the area, "where's Cat?"

"She went home last night." From the corner of his eye, Josef saw Wayne shaking his head from side to side, cautioning Dale.

"Do you want someone to look at your place?" Dale asked.

"No, thanks. I've got my insurance agent coming to take a look. The front of my house, garage and truck are the only things I can see that have damage. Of course, I'll have to have him take a look at this place, too. Now that it's mine."

The three men walked through the debris field toward the sheds. Josef's heart sank. Sank for Cat. The only remainders of the barn and house were the stone foundations and a few partial walls.

"Foundations." He whispered the word and then with the thought and possibilities, his voice rose in excitement. "We have foundations."

"Joe?" Wayne touched his arm. "You all right?"

"Yeah, fine." He was fine. "I need to make some calls. Thanks for the help. I'll see you later." He and Cat had a stone foundation just like the house and barn. They had something to build on. Together. He loved her and wanted her to be a part of his life.

Rescue Me

* * * *

"Can I use the bathroom?" Wayne asked, stepping onto the porch.

"You know where it is." Josef struggled to put the plastic over the broken window.

A few minutes later he heard, "You gonna be a daddy?"

His stomach flutter. "What are ya talking 'bout? No."

"Are you sure? There's a pregnancy test lodged in the sink drain. Somehow in that storm it never blew away. Must be a sign. I didn't pick it up, but you might want to."

Josef jumped from the ladder and ran into the bathroom. The flutter turned to a flock of birds flying in his gut.

"So?" Wayne stood in the bathroom doorway.

"It's blank. Where are the instructions?" He grabbed the box on the floor and like a fanatic heroine read the back. She could be pregnant with his baby. "It's blank. It states to retake the test. Or it might be too early."

"Do you want me to call Jackson?"

"No," he yelled. "I don't want anyone to know." He glared at Wayne. "You understand?"

"Jesus. Yeah, I got it. Mouth shut." Wayne pinched his thumb and forefinger together and zipped his lips shut with the imaginary zipper.

"I'll handle this." Josef threw the test in the garbage and carried the box into the kitchen.

"I didn't know you two had that kind of relationship again." Wayne wiggled his eyebrows.

"Shut up. One night. That's all." One night of heaven. He wanted to experience it all over again and again and again.

"That's all it takes to become a daddy."

"Shut up." He shoved Wayne back and dialed the phone. *Why didn't she say anything about the test?*

"She didn't answer?" Wayne stated as Josef shoved his cell phone in his pocket.

"No," he said short and clipped, returning to the porch to finish working with the plastic cover.

"Let me help you get the plastic up, and I'll leave."

"Grab an end and pull tight while sticking the plastic to the tape."

They worked in silence until the plastic was adhered to the four

113

broken windows.

Wayne pulled keys from his front pocket. "Poker Tuesday night?"

"I'll be there. Thanks for helping and putting up with my temper."

"Not a problem. That's what I came for. See ya Tuesday."

As Wayne walked away, Josef started the blow dryer to finish the covering process. He mumbled angrily while he worked. "She didn't trust me to tell me she took a test. She trusted me enough, to remind me we didn't use protection though. Can I trust her to tell me whether or not she's carrying my child?"

Yes, she would tell him. Cat wasn't the kind to keep secrets.

* * * *

Josef continued calling Cat throughout the day. It had been a struggle to focus on things needing to get done. Now sitting on the porch step, with dusk settling upon the land, he looked across the road at what used to be Elaine's house and tried Cat's cell phone again.

"Hello?" a woman's voice answered but not Cat.

"Hi, Margaret. Is Cat available?" The flutter returned to his stomach, happy to finally get through.

"Josef?"

"Yes."

"Just a minute." Her voiced was muffled, but he heard, "You need to talk to him. Catherine Elaine, you can't run away from this."

Silence.

"What?" Her sharp tone cut deep.

"When were you going to tell me?" He didn't mean to bark the question at her, but her attitude and the situation at hand didn't help matters. His leg bounced with nervous energy.

"Tell you what?"

He took a calming breath. "Are you pregnant?"

He heard her breathing and then Margaret's voice. "Josef, what did you say to her?"

"I asked her a question. Please put her back on."

Margaret's subdued voice said, "He wants to talk to you. Go to your room if you need privacy."

The line remained quiet. He waited. Footsteps and then a door closed.

"I don't know," came the whisper of her voice.

"Why didn't you tell me?" A lump formed in his throat.

"Tell you what? You knew there was a chance." There was doubt in her voice.

He swallowed. "Wayne found the test—"

"Shit! I forgot about it with the tornado and everything. If Wayne knows then—" Doubt turned to panic.

"No one else will know." Both legs bounced out of control. "I'll kill him if he tells anyone, and he knows it. I looked at the test, but it was blank."

"I think it's too early. I need to wait until after I'm supposed to … that time of the month."

He stood and paced the porch. "That's midweek right?" He remembered their discussion at his parent's house about the situation.

"Yes. Listen Josef, you don't need to worry about it." Her tone hardened. "I'm sure I'm not, and if I am, well then I'll deal with it."

"Deal with it?" His voice rose and cracked. "What the hell is that supposed to mean?"

"When the contract you have for farming on my land is up, I won't be renegotiating. I'm going to build on it." Her voice frosted the beer he iced earlier.

"I don't give a *shit* about the land." He didn't care for her cold tone or attitude or choice. "I love you, and if you're pregnant with my baby, then I'll have a say about it." The lump reformed in his throat. His heart pounded against his chest like a rubber mallet. His eyes moistened, and tears formed.

"I know the history of the farm. I know … I need to go."

"Cat, don't. Please." He pleaded with tears streaming down his cheeks.

"Goodbye." The line went dead.

She was gone.

Again.

* * * *

Catherine sat on the edge of the bed. Josef knew about the test and would be waiting. Waiting for an answer. Waiting to find out whether they would be parents or not. She wouldn't be a burden to him if the test came back positive. She could handle this on her own. Abortion wasn't an option. There were plenty of single mothers in the world, and they were surviving.

Why did he tell her he loved her? Was he serious? What about the land? To tell her he didn't care about it ... he had to be lying. She knew how much he wanted the land. She knew how much the land meant to him. The only thing he had right was having some sort of say about the baby, *if* she were pregnant.

She surveyed her old bedroom. Not much changed from her high school years other than the rock bands and animal posters had been removed from the plum painted walls. Black drapes hung from the windows, her favorite books sat on the wood shelves she painted black and stuffed animals sat in a corner. It was dark and uninviting.

"Mom," she yelled after opening the door. "We need to redo my room. It's too dark."

"What? What's gotten into you, Catherine?"

She came down the stairs into the kitchen to see her mom's face scrunched in confusion.

"It's just that, while sitting in my room, I didn't like how confining it felt."

"I like your room the way it is. It's a great room to sleep in. Nice and dark. You close those drapes and barely any light comes through."

"You sleep in there?"

"Sometimes your father snores so bad, I have to leave. Your room is the perfect escape." Margaret checked the sauce simmering. "Now what was all that about with Joe?"

"Nothing."

"It's *something* because you didn't want to talk to him, and when you did, you froze up. What did he say to you?"

"Mom, I don't want to talk about it. It's nothing." Catherine filled the large pot with hot water for the pasta noodles.

"Fine. You don't want to talk to your mother, maybe you'll talk to your sister."

"It's nothing. And I won't be talking to her. Or my brothers either."

She set the pot on the gas stovetop and turned the burner on. "Okay?"

"Okay. So tell me, why did you say yes to Joe?"

"I don't want to talk about this." Agitated, she stomped to the stairs.

"You need to think about it, Catherine." Margaret stated to her retreating back.

Catherine closed the door, sat on her bed and let the darkness surround her. Why *did* she say yes? Wasn't she marrying him for the barn and money? Yes. So what difference was there between her reason for marriage and Josef's reason? None. There was no reason to marry at all. The barn was gone. The horses were without a home.

But a baby could change everything. She would have to give up the rescue operation because the time would be spent with the baby instead of the horses. There would be attorney fees to pay to settle the custody of the baby between Josef and her. Taking money away from the horses.

Yup, a baby would change everything.

Chapter Seventeen

The insurance agent left Josef's Monday afternoon. With Elaine's farm clear of debris—much of it bulldozed into a pile, Josef made what would be called an 'executive decision'. He didn't know who Cat had decided on for the barn remodeling, so he made a call to Rangston Builders. They came highly recommended by some friends who owned a horse ranch south of the cities. The company agreed to send out a contractor to evaluate the job that afternoon since Josef said he wanted the construction done as soon as possible.

A truck with the Rangston logo on the door pulled up mid-afternoon. "Josef?" the contractor said, getting out of his truck. "Bob Thompson. A pleasure to meet you." They shook hands.

"You, too. I'm hoping you'll be able to get started on this job ASAP," Josef said with a glance toward Elaine's home.

"What are we talking about?"

"Let's go over there." Josef gestured and started crossing the road to Elaine's farm. "I recently inherited this property only to have a tornado destroy the house and barn."

"Sorry to hear that."

"As ya can see, I have the foundation for the house." He pointed in the direction of the barn. "And over this way the barn's foundation. I have to have a new barn, but the house isn't needed. I'd like to keep the cost below fifty grand, but my max is a hundred thousand."

The contractor's eyebrows arched as his eyes widened. "What kind of barn? And how big?"

"It must have at least four stalls and whatever else needed for a horse barn. I want an office, maybe the same size as a stall, with water and electricity, which is already here on the property."

Bob jotted notes in a portfolio. "You'll want a wash-down stall and a place to store tack. Do you want a place for hay or feed storage?"

"I got that covered. Wait, I take that back, add a place for hay bales."

"What are you thinking material-wise?"

"I want wood to be the primary material. It needs to be painted red." He wanted Cat to be reminded of the old place. "Listen, I don't know a lot about horse barns, but I trust you'll come up with something spectacular. I want this barn to last a hundred years."

"Didn't you tell the office there was a short timeline on this job? How soon are we talking?"

"The sooner the better. I'd love to see you start tomorrow." Josef laughed at the impossibility.

"Well, it won't be that soon." Bob laughed with him. "I need to draw up plans, get your approval, building permits, prepare the area and get the materials. We're looking at a month minimum before we can get started. My guys could be up earlier to start clearing the area." Bob strolled around the concrete foundation with Josef following. "To be honest, I'd like to work with a flat surface. Do you want the new barn in the same spot?"

"Yes. If possible, I'd like the concrete bricks saved for my use. Your men can pile them up over by what's remaining of the sheds there." Josef pointed to the left where his tractor sat parked under the green steel walls of what used to be a building.

"Okay. What about fencing outside of the barn?"

"I can take care of that. So, how soon can I see plans to get them approved?"

The contractor repeated his list, and Josef nodded in agreement. "Wednesday would be the earliest, but no later than Friday."

"I look forward to hearing from you."

The two walked across the road. As the contractor got into his pickup, Josef said, "Your guys can come at any time to get started. Remember, the sooner the better for me."

With a nod the contractor left, and Josef thought about Cat. The possibility of being a father grew on him. He missed having her in the house. Even Blonde missed her and the dogs. Seeing her smile and hearing her laugh. His love for her renewed, he'd get her back to the farm to show her the barn being constructed.

To convince her to stay.

To ask her to be a part of his life.

To be his wife.

* * * *

Wednesday came and went with no sign of her period. By Friday morning, still no sign. After much contemplation, Cat would wait until after work. If the test were positive, she'd never be able to focus on her job, where being attentive was crucial.

Home from work Friday evening, Cat put the dogs out and fed the cats. She pulled the box from the drugstore bag and stared at the pregnancy test. She went to her bedroom, sat on the edge of the bed and read the instructions carefully.

The instructions stated it was best to take the test in the morning when hormone levels were higher. Not wanting to wait any longer, she went into the bathroom and followed the directions. She set the test on the counter. Washing shaking hands, she glanced to where the test sat.

Two faint pink lines.

Her heart weighed heavy in her chest.

The two lines grew dark pink as the seconds past.

She grabbed the instruction sheet to verify what she already knew. Slowly she sank onto the closed toilet lid. She was disappointed for giving in to her need to satisfy her body's wanting Josef. Angry for not remembering to use protection. Scared knowing she carried a child that would be dependent on her.

The test proved she was having Josef's baby. The joy and elation weren't there. *Now to tell Josef.* She needed to think.

She gradually rose, threw the test away, and changed out of her work clothes. Not wanting to eat, she brought the dogs inside, then took them to the truck. The horses would be therapeutic for her, and so would the workout she'd get while mucking the stalls.

Due to the enormity of the situation, she would take her time before

Rescue Me

telling Josef about the baby. Time for her to absorb the reality of the situation. Time for her to make plans. Time for her to be honest with herself.

* * * *

Cat went through the motions of cleaning the stalls while her head churned questions of what would happen. What would happen to the horses? She had nine months to figure out that one. What would happen with her career? Nothing. She needed money to support her and the baby. How was she going to tell Josef? How was she going to tell her parents? But more importantly, what did *she* want? Good question. There was no going backward, only forward. One day at a time.

First things first, schedule a doctor's appointment to confirm the results. There could always be the possibility of a false-positive test. Right? She had to be sure. One-hundred-percent-doctor-proven-sure before she told anyone.

"Evening, Catherine." She jumped at Warren's voice. "Sorry, didn't mean to startle you. You all right?"

"I'm fine. Just a lot on my mind these days." She led Churchill into the barn. "I'm still in search of a place for the horses. I would really like to avoid putting them in a boarding facility but may have to."

"Well, what would you say if I told you the new owners of this place visited while you were at your aunt's and asked about the horses?"

She closed the stall gate. "I'll have them off the property in time." A breeze from nowhere blew up her back and over her shoulders.

"No, they wanted to know what you used them for. I explained your rescue mission to them. Then they asked if they were for sale."

Catherine's heart galloped with mixed emotions, knowing there would come a time to let them go. "What did you tell them?" Wheelbarrow in hand, she sauntered toward the doors.

"I said as far as I knew they were, but they'd have to talk to you. I gave them your name and number, so maybe you'll have one less horse to move."

"Maybe." A slight sadness filled her heart. Yet it opened a window of hope and opportunity with the baby. "Thanks, Warren. Hey, how are things in the packing world?" She parked the wheelbarrow in the corner and stepped outside of the barn.

"Good. I'm having an auction to get rid of all the things I'm not taking with me. I don't need much where I'm going. Just glad Rufus gets to move with me. Otherwise, I would've asked you to take him. Just what you would've wanted or needed—another mouth to feed."

Another mouth to feed. Ha. Her mental voice cracked as she hollered for the dogs to get in the truck's cab. Her eyes moistened, and the tears were on the edge of breaking the dam.

She cleared her throat while situating herself behind the steering wheel. "Thanks again, Warren, for everything."

"My pleasure. Night now." He waved as she drove off.

About a quarter mile away from Warren's place, Catherine pulled off the road and let the tears spill free. She didn't want to be pregnant. Not now. Her career was solid. The rescue operation was under way. And to be honest she just wasn't ready to become a single mother.

She couldn't wait for the doctor visit. She wiped the tears away and pulled onto the road. Instead of going home, she'd make a quick stop at the drug store to buy another test to take in the morning.

* * * *

Unable to sleep Saturday morning, Catherine woke early and went into the bathroom. Two boxes sitting on the countertop stared at her. Two different brands of pregnancy tests. She ripped open one box, took the test out and did the same with the other box. With a quick read through the instructions, she did what was needed and waited.

One test took a minute to pop up the pink lettering 'PREGNANT.' The other test turned into a bright pink plus sign as well.

"Shit." Her stomach churned.

No denying it at this point. Two tests—no, make that three—all showed positive. She was pregnant. She was going to be a mom. She was going to have Josef's baby.

Catherine turned off the bathroom light and crawled back into bed. Four o'clock in the morning was too early to be up on a day off. Plus, she wasn't ready to face the world. Or more truthfully that she was having a baby.

Little Buddy hopped on the bed and nudged her hand.

"Hey, Buddy." She stroked the cat's soft fur, and the tension in her body eased a bit.

Tonight was family night at Mom and Dad's. She looked forward to a good home cooked meal. She closed her eyes and wondered what carrying a child was going to feel like. She remembered how wonderful Maureen looked at the lake and how happy she was.

Catherine wanted that happiness.

Chapter Eighteen

Josef pulled to the curb in front of the house matching the house number and description Margaret gave. When he couldn't get through to Cat on the phone Friday, he contacted Margaret to see if she knew where Cat was and why she didn't answer her phone. Margaret invited him to dinner, and he agreed, unable to turn her down because Cat would be at the house.

Cat's truck sat parked in the driveway among multiple vehicles. He didn't know the entire family would be there, but then again he didn't care. He had to know if she was carrying his child. He had to know if he was going to be a father.

He approached the front door and heard laughter. With a deep breath, he pushed the doorbell and heard, "Catherine, would you get that."

The door opened. A startled gasp escaped her lungs while she placed a hand upon his chest pushing him back. "What are you doing here?"

It was obvious Margaret hadn't told her he was coming.

"Your mother invited me."

"She what? Why would she do that?"

Cat looked beautiful even if she was angry. Her eyes sparkled, and her skin flushed.

"You wouldn't answer or return my calls. I called your mother, and before I knew it she invited me for dinner." He reached to touch her. To feel her again.

But she pulled away before he could skim her skin. "You called my mom?" she questioned with a raised voice and then lowered to a near growl. "What did you tell her?"

"I didn't say anything other than I was trying to reach you, and you weren't getting back to me." He stared into chestnut eyes. "We need to talk."

The door flew open. "Josef," Margaret exclaimed. "You made it. Come on in. Catherine, let him in."

"I didn't *know* he was the surprise guest this evening, *Mother*."

Josef stepped past Catherine into the house where talking and laughter flowed through the open patio door. Cat's graduation was the last time he had seen her sister and brothers.

"Did you have any troubles finding the house?" Margaret took him by the arm and led him through a large living room.

"Nope. You have a lovely home."

"Thank you." She continued through a large kitchen and out a patio door to an enormous deck with a lower level patio. "Everyone, look who's here."

He was inundated with manly hugs by Cat's three brothers—Mike Jr., Frank and Mark—then a gentler hug from her sister Sophia. Cat hung back during the introductions.

"This is my wife Audrey," Mike Jr. spoke first. "And the lone girl out running with the boys is our daughter Emily. She's nine. And the boy with the crew cut and striped tee shirt is our four-year-old son Adam. And hopefully within the year we can announce number three." Mike earned a slap in the arm by his wife.

Josef smiled and wondered if he'd be announcing his first anytime soon, but didn't get long to think about it because Frank spoke next.

"This is Brooke." Frank hugged the little girl next to him. "And that other little munchkin is ours. His name's Hunter, and he just turned five."

"Mark, Sophia and Catherine have yet to marry," Margaret stated, "before I see any grandchildren from them."

"You won't have to wait that long." Cat blurted, and all eyes fell upon her. "I …" She ran into the house, and all eyes swiveled to Josef.

Josef didn't say anything. He didn't know what to do. Thank God his body knew what to do. Veins pumped blood as fast as his heart raced it out. Did her comment mean what he thought it meant? Should he go after her? His ears roared with the pulsating of blood rushing through his veins.

He turned and stepped inside after Cat but stopped, not sure where to go.

"Her room's up the stairs," Margaret spoke from the doorway. "On the left."

He nodded and ran up the short flight of stairs. To the left he stood in front of a closed door. His life could change forever when he entered the room. He inhaled deeply and exhaled slowly.

With a light knock, he turned the knob and entered darkness. "Cat?" He closed the door. She was crying softly. "Can we talk?" At that moment, he was mad for not having brought the engagement ring.

"I didn't mean to blurt it out." Her confession came through snivels.

He followed her voice ahead and a little to the left to the bed. Sitting on the edge his eyes adjusted to the darkness. "You don't need to apologize. Does it mean what I think? Are we—? Are you—?"

"Yes." A sniffle came from the darkness. "I'm pregnant. You're going to be a father."

He was going to be a daddy. His heart beat quickened, and his insides bounced around elated. He reached to locate her, to comfort her. "Where are you? It's so damned dark in here."

A giggle was followed by another sniffle. That was a good sign.

"I'm serious. I can't see a damned thing."

There was movement on the bed, and a warm hand touched his arm. He wanted to hug and hold her but didn't dare push things.

"I didn't call or answer because I knew you'd want to know. I wasn't sure until this morning. I took two more tests, and both were positive. No question about it." She leaned against his back, and warmth spread throughout his body.

"What are your plans? And I don't mean ... I guess I want to know where I fit into all of this."

"There's no question about anything. I'm having the baby. You're the father. We'll figure the rest out when the time comes."

He turned. "Do the right thing, Cat. Marry me."

"The right thing?"

The heat radiating off her body no longer lingered on him.

"I'm not going to marry you. We've been through this once already, and I'm not going to discuss it again. You lied to me."

"When you want something so bad and really feel it should be yours, you'd do anything to make that happen. I was doing what I thought I needed to. Don't you understand? You wanted it as bad as I did and lied to me, too."

She stopped crying. Her voice raised an angered octave. "When did I lie?"

"College. You never told me the truth about why you broke up with me. You lied to me. You cheated on me. On us."

Silence.

"I'm sorry." Her voice came soft. "But it doesn't change anything. If you want, I'll sell you the land."

"I don't want the land. I want you. Things have changed. I've changed."

He couldn't say anything more. He didn't want to say anything more for fear of saying the wrong thing. He needed to leave. He needed to think things through. One thing was certain—he loved her. They both needed space and time.

He stood, walked to the door, and stopped. "I'll be in touch." He opened the door, and the light shone on her lying curled in a fetal position. "I love you, Cat." He closed the door and left with a heavy heart.

* * * *

"Crap!" Catherine slammed her fist into the mattress. "Now what? Nothing like making me feel like shit. What nerve. To leave telling me he loves me? Bullshit!" A pillow over her head, she screamed as loud as possible.

A knock and her mother's voice on the other side of the door had her stopping, putting the pillow behind her head.

"Catherine, can I come in?" Margaret asked.

"Yes," she said in a clipped tone and turned on the bedside light. "Sorry. I didn't mean to snip at you." She sat against the pillows.

Her mom filled Josef's void. "Where's Josef?"

"I think he left. We had an argument."

"Would you like to talk about it?"

"Not really, Mom." She turned and curled up.

"Is there anything you want to tell me?"

"Mom, please. Not now. Can you give me a few minutes?"

"Okay." Her mom went to the door. "Dad's grilling now. We should be eating in about ten minutes."

"Thanks." Her mom must've guessed about the pregnancy but thankfully didn't press the subject. She hoped the rest of the family wouldn't say anything.

The dark room had been a nice cover during her confrontation with Josef. If they could've seen each other, she wasn't sure how she would've responded to him. She wanted to go into his arms but couldn't lead him on.

She meant it when she told him she'd sell the land to him. As much as she loved the farm and all the memories, if she built on the land, seeing him every day would be painful. Yet she would be reminded of him every time she looked at her child. Their child. His and her child. A child made from love.

"Oh. My. God." Catherine jumped from the bed and ran from her room to the living room.

Cell phone in hand, she hustled out the front door to have privacy while making the call.

"Catherine, what's going on? What are you doing out here?" her mom asked from the front door. Cat raised a hand and waved her off.

No answer. Either Josef couldn't hear the phone, or he didn't want to talk to her. She wouldn't blame him. After the way she announced the pregnancy to him, in front of her family, hell, she'd be mad too.

He told her several times in the past week he loved her, but how much of the love was real? She had heard the phone conversation—he wanted the land. Then later he told her he loved her and things had changed. That he loved her. But could she trust him? With her life? Yes. With love?

She ended the call when voicemail played. The answer to her last questionable thought, could she could trust him in love, had come to her … slowly but it came eventually. It was she who shouldn't be trusted. It was she who had cheated on him and their relationship. It was she who should crawl back, asking for forgiveness.

Instead she crept into the house and returned the phone to her purse. The family gathered in the kitchen and filled their plates full of all her favorite summer grilling foods. Hamburgers and brats with all the fixings, grilled veggies, baked beans, potato salad, coleslaw, potato chips and fresh cut up fruit.

Mark, her younger brother, stated, "So you have a bun in the oven, huh," when she entered the room.

"Mark," her mom quickly scolded. "If Catherine has news to share, she'll share it when she's ready."

"Thanks, Mom." She filled her plate and sat at the enormous patio table. When everyone was seated, she said loudly, "I *do* have an announcement." All but her niece and nephews who sat at a small children's picnic table quieted. "Josef and I are expecting. I haven't been to the doctor but have taken three tests."

"Three?" Mark snickered, earning a glare of threatened death from his mother. "Sorry. Congratulations."

The rest of the family followed Mark's lead with congratulations. Her mom followed with, "When is the wedding?"

"I don't know if there'll be one." She shoved the hamburger in her mouth and took a bite.

"What did Josef say?" Her mom continued with the questioning … which Catherine expected.

"He just found out tonight. He left after we argued. I don't want to talk about this right now. This is between me and him." A spoonful of baked beans went in her mouth this time. Anything to avoid further conversation … especially this particular one.

Her father spoke with a stern voice. "You can't have a baby and not be married. You and Josef will be married before the baby arrives."

"Mike," her mom warned her father.

"I will not let my daughter have a child out of wedlock." Her father was firm, serious and not to be crossed.

"You can't force the two of them into marriage if they don't want too. Single women are having babies every day and successfully raising children. I'm sure they'll do the right thing. Now let's enjoy this wonderful dinner."

Catherine ate without being bombarded by further questions, but she saw the love mixed with hurt in her father's eyes. Thoughts bounced in her head along with a long list of things to do in the next nine months. Tonight she would cross one of the items off that list.

Chapter Nineteen

Josef dialed the number, started the truck and pulled from the curb. He didn't say goodbye to Cat's family because the questions would create conflict. Plus Cat didn't want him around.

He was going to be a father. He smiled, but it quickly faded. He wanted to marry Cat. Not because it was the right thing to do because of the baby but because he loved her.

"Rangston Builders. This is Bob."

"Bob, this is Josef Garrison."

"Josef, what can I do for you?"

"I'm wondering if I can offer an incentive to move this project along a little faster?" He navigated his way through the neighborhood streets toward the freeway.

"I'm working on things as quickly as possible. With your approval Wednesday on the plans, I filed paperwork for permits and ordered supplies on Friday. I can send the guys out on Tuesday to start prepping?"

"That would be fantastic. Anything to show some forward progress." Josef couldn't contain his excitement.

"If you don't mind my asking, why the rush?"

"I'm having this built for … I'm hoping a woman will say yes to a marriage proposal based on what you're doing."

"Wow. That's some engagement gift."

"Don't you know it! So listen, if you and your men can have this project finished in a month's time from permit approval, I'll give you an additional two thousand."

"Won't and can't take the money, Josef. It's not needed. We'll get this done for you."

"Thank you. You've made my day."

"My pleasure."

The men hung up, and Josef tossed the phone in the console. He turned the radio up and headed north for home. Next week he'd send Cat flowers, and once things took shape with the barn, he'd call and persuade her to pay him a visit. Unless she called first. Which he highly doubted. She needed time to adjust to their situation and the changes her body would be going through. Hell, he needed a little time to adjust.

Blondie barked wildly as he pulled into the drive. He opened the truck door, and she placed her paws on his thigh. "Hey, girl," he greeted, rubbing her head. "I need something to eat." They entered the kitchen. "Missed out on dinner. We're gonna have a baby in the house. What do you think about that, girl?" Nothing could wipe the smile from his face.

Blondie gave a quick bark, ran into the living room and back, and dropped one of her stuffed toys at his feet.

"Aren't you sweet," he laughed at the dog. "I don't think the baby will want your drool soaked stuffed bunny."

"Rrrruff," Blondie responded before she picked up the animal and trotted into the other room.

Josef chuckled and opened the refrigerator to find something to eat. Tonight he'd settle for a sandwich, chips and an ice-cold beer on the patio.

On his third beer with an action flick on TV, he settled on the couch with Blondie at his feet. The dog's ears perked up. She got up and trotted to the front door. Headlights bounced off the entry walls.

"It's just someone needing to turn around. Come back and relax."

The dog's tail wagged in a frenzy as she barked.

He walked to the door to see who it could be. A silver pickup drove up his driveway. His heart raced with anticipation. It was her. Cat was coming to him. Out the front door, down the porch steps and to the truck he ran.

Josef ran toward her, wearing a big dumbass ear-to-ear grin, and he didn't care.

"Don't say anything." She and the dogs hopped out. Blondie was excited to have her playmates back. "I have questions you need to answer."

"Okay, anything." His breathing came quick. "Do ya want to sit out on the porch or inside?" His heart thudded hard enough he could feel the rush in his ears.

"The porch would be nice."

"Can I get ya something to drink?"

"Water's fine since I can't have a beer," she whined, and he chuckled. "Laugh all you want. If I can't have it, you can't have it either."

He stopped laughing and walking, said, "I'm not the one pregnant. I can drink alcohol. *You* can't."

"If I can't, you can't." Her eyebrows raised, and her eyes didn't waver from his while saying it. She was serious.

"Okay, deal, but can I at least finish the bottle I have open?" He fell into step next to her and gestured at the house.

"Drink it slow and enjoy every last barley-and-hops-filled swig." A smirk returned to her face, and a warm feeling filled his gut.

"I'll be back with our beverages." He went inside, grabbed a bottled water from the fridge and his bottle of beer from the table in the living room. At least the beer was a fresh bottle, giving him more to enjoy. "Here ya go." He handed her the water while he leaned against the railing in front of where Cat sat.

"Thanks. I want to know if you trust me." She took a drink.

"Why wouldn't I?"

"Because of what I did when we were dating in college." Her eyes fell to her feet.

"That was years ago. It hurt at first to hear you tell me, but I understand. We weren't together. We were separated by distance." He sat next to her. Gently with a finger he lifted her chin and turned her face to look him in the eye. "Yes, I trust you. Or is there something else I should know?" He took a pull from the beer bottle.

"No. That's what I needed to hear."

"Do you trust *me*?" Josef asked without looking at her.

"Yes, but I want the truth about that phone call."

"What phone …? Oh, the one you overheard." He took a steadying breath because this had to be said right, or she'd be gone. "Please hear me out. I did want the land. For years I felt that my family should get it back in the family. I thought if I could show Elaine how much I appreciated and worked hard with the land, she'd will it to me.

"You came back, and I worried. Worried she'd see you in need and give it all to you. Worried about old feelings which I fought. I didn't want to admit that I still had strong feelings for you.

"The surprise—and shock of the will hit me hard. I didn't understand why. We already talked about why we were going to get married. What you didn't know was that I planned on divorcing you after you got all the money."

Her mouth dropped opened.

"I wouldn't have taken any of the money in the divorce, but would've fought for the land and the land only. It was all I wanted. *Was.* Like I said back at your parents, you want something so bad you start believing that it should be yours, and you'd do anything to get it. That was then. *Was.*"

"But now?"

"Cat, I love you." His large hands engulfed hers. "I have always loved you. I don't care about the land. I care about you. I care about our baby." He moved their hands to her belly. "*Our* baby. I'll be right back." Josef jogged inside to the china cabinet, opened the drawer and grabbed the black velvet box and his laptop.

"What are you doing with your laptop?" Although she smiled, her eyebrows pinched together in confusion.

"I need to show ya something. But first," Josef got down onto one knee. "Catherine, will you marry me?"

"Yes, I'll marry you."

He slid the ring on her finger, and she pulled him to her lips. He kept the kiss short. He sat next to her with the laptop. "Now to show you." He tapped the keyboard. "They'll start working Tuesday to prep the land for building." He slid the computer to her lap, and she stared at the screen.

"What is it? I can see it's blueprints, but of what?"

"Your new barn. For the horses. For you."

"Oh my, Josef. You did all of this for me?"

"For us. For our future." He placed the laptop on the bench and embraced her. Their lips touched, tongues danced, and his body came to life. This time it was him who wanted her. He slapped the laptop closed and quickly filled his hand with her backside.

"Let's go to bed." He scooped her up in his arms and carried her there.

He placed a delicate kiss on her lips. "I love you." He stated the words with honesty and passion and didn't allow a moment for a reply. He feverishly took her mouth with kisses of want and slid to her side.

Hands wandered to waistlines. Tops flew to the floor, and her bra landed somewhere over his head in the room. Her hands moved to the button of his shorts. He took them in his and shook his head. Releasing his hold, his hand slowly maneuvered and undid her shorts. He scooted his large six-foot plus frame down where he positioned himself over her legs in a kneeling position.

The kiss was gentle and filled with love as he placed it on her belly where their baby was cocooned. He trailed the kisses up to her breasts, taking one nipple at a time and heightened their peak. She withered beneath him. He moved kisses to her collarbone, up her neck, stopped to nibble on her ear and returned to her delectable mouth.

His hand moved between skin and panties where he found her moist center. She arched her back at his touch and moaned. He couldn't take it any longer. His body ached for her touch. For her feel. For her warmth.

He pulled her shorts off and let her hands take care of removing his. Her hand wrapped around the length of his manhood, and a moan of ecstasy escaped. Cat pushed him to his back, straddled him as her warmth slowly surrounded him. He gripped the sheets as she rode and teased his manhood for what seemed like hours.

They rolled over. He was in charge and charge he did. Her body shuddered. His release of rapture followed, then he collapsed at her side. "Are you okay?"

"Couldn't be better," she said through heavy breaths. "Thank you." She rolled to her side, backing up against him.

He placed his arm over her waist, and his hand spread the width of her flat tummy. Soon it would be growing and moving with their child. Josef smiled at the mere thought, kissed Cat's neck and whispered, "I love you."

She echoed his words of endearment.

He pulled up the sheets covering their naked bodies, gathered her into his body and held her. "I'm glad you came. I mean here. To me."

"I'm glad for both," she laughed.

"Let's go tell my parents the news tomorrow." Excited like a child on Christmas morning he couldn't wait to share the news. "They would be home from church by the time we get there. I know you need to get home, too, so we'll both drive."

"Shouldn't we call first?"

"No, Sundays are always an open invitation at their house. More so during the summer months because of the lake. So are ya up for it?"

"Yeah, but aren't you going to church?"

"No. I think the Lord will understand, but Father Tim may not. He won't be happy to hear the news of our marriage or the expected baby." A sad-sounding laugh escaped him.

"You think he'll be that disappointed?"

"He was expecting the church to receive the trust fund. Yes, he'll be upset."

Cat's face turned serious. "I know he's said he won't marry us, but what about the baby being baptized?"

"We'll cross that bridge after we're married. If it means leaving the church and going elsewhere, then so be it. Enough of this conversation. Let's get some sleep."

"I don't want to sleep." Turning in his arms, her breast rubbed against his chest, and her lips took possession of his mouth.

A-tten-tion! His manhood came to life in the palm of her hand.

Chapter Twenty

Catherine parked behind Josef, who was out of his vehicle and there to open her door. "Thank you. It looks like we weren't the only ones who decided to visit your folks."

"I kinda figured Adam and Maureen would be here. She loves the water. You two will have a lot to talk about." He squeezed her at the waist. "And it looks like John and Tiff are here, too."

All the dogs relieved themselves and raced for the front door. Even Fritz joined in the frolic. He had healed and adjusted well to his surroundings.

Entering the quiet house, Josef headed for the bar fridge.

"No alcohol. Water only. Remember?"

"You're gonna be on me like a hound on a scent trail."

"You got that right." She howled like a hound dog and followed the noise with a grin.

"Two waters coming up." He handed her a bottle. "Let's go tell the family our great news." Josef's smile lit up his eyes with happiness, warming her heart.

They walked through the patio door, and the dogs ran for the lake. "No," Catherine yelled, but it was too late. "I guess I'll drive home with the windows down."

"Catherine! Josef!" Barbara yelled, surprised and happy.

"Hi, Mom."

"Hello, Josef. Does this mean what I think it means?" Barbara embraced both.

"Yes," Cat stepped from the hug and wiggling her fingers to show

137

the engagement ring was back where it belonged.

"Oh goody! Now your mother and I can make plans."

"Mom, slow down. First Cat and I have more to talk about."

Maureen came out of the lake wearing a bikini, and Catherine couldn't help but stare at her large pregnant belly. How quickly would her baby grow, changing the shape of her body?

"It's good to see you again, Catherine. Did you bring a suit? The lake feels great." Maureen approached the seating area.

"No suit. This was a last minute trip. You look fantastic."

She carefully lowered her bulky body into a chair. "Thanks, but I'm ready for this to be over with. I want my body back."

Catherine chuckled and wondered if she'd feel the same way. Hell, or look half as good as Maureen. She seemed tiny for being nine months along. As cute as Maureen was, no way would she be caught dead in a bikini while nine months pregnant.

"Since everyone's here, Cat and I wanted to share the exciting news." Josef glanced her way, and she nodded. "We're having a baby."

The men congratulated Josef, and the women squealed, piercing the afternoon air. Barbara embraced Cat while Maureen slowly hefted her pregnant body from the chair.

"I knew it. When you didn't feel good on the Fourth, I knew it." Barbara stepped back, eyeing Catherine's belly. "It will be so nice to have grandbabies only nine months apart. They're going to be such great friends."

Maureen hugged her. "Congratulations on all accounts. It will be fun having kids close in age. How are you feeling?"

"So far I'm fine. No complaints. I still need to go to the doctor, but three home tests showing positive is pretty convincing for me." Catherine was excited and ready to start a new life with Josef, the farm and their baby.

"I should go through my maternity clothes for you. I may have stuff that would work for this season."

"That would be great. Thank you."

"So we're going to have a wedding sooner rather than later. Right?" Barbara stated.

"Mom, enough. Cat and I haven't had a chance to talk about it. I do have the marriage license though." He glanced at Cat, warming her cheeks, reminding her of the events from a few short weeks ago.

"I need to take care of things back in the cities before I can focus on a wedding and the baby."

"Fine. No wedding talk for now. I'm going to get lunch ready. You girls stay right here." Barbara strolled toward the house.

The women chatted about pregnancy, babies and all the necessities needed for their arrival. Tiffany listened as Maureen and Catherine talked baby talk and asked, "I get to babysit, right?"

Maureen was quick to reply. "Most definitely!"

"I'm sure we'll be in need, too, but I think you're going to have stiff competition from Grandma." Catherine laughed along with Maureen and Tiffany.

"Time for lunch," Barbara yelled from the deck.

"Ladies first." Josef waited for Catherine, and they loitered to the deck stairs together. "I thought that went well."

"I didn't imagine it would go any other way." She smiled, happy with how smoothly things were going. She loved this man and their baby. Her smile grew with the thought of Elaine and her ghostly *visit*. Elaine had told her everything would be all right.

"The dogs shouldn't smell after their baths, but they may be a little wet still." Josef held Cat beside her pickup. He didn't want to let her go but would have the rest of his life with her by his side.

"I'll take clean wet over stinky lake wet any day. Thank your mom again for lunch. We should start making plans for the wedding. The sooner the better. I have a few thoughts."

"You do, huh?" Their bodies caressed as he pulled her in closer. "How about a honeymoon? Have ya thought about that?" He wiggled his eyebrows.

"I don't think we'll be doing a honeymoon anytime soon. I'll be so busy moving and with the baby—"

"No using the baby as an excuse. We'll have a honeymoon. Maybe not right away, but we'll have a honeymoon."

"Okay. Just don't make any set plans until after I'm settled. I need to get going. I'll call you when I get home."

"I'll be waiting. I love you."

He kissed her, and she got in the truck.

"I love you." A warm feeling came over him. He closed her door and she drove away.

* * * *

"Hello," Josef answered the ringing phone, surprised to see Margaret's name on his screen.

"Josef, Catherine's been in an accident."

His heart stopped and fell to the pit of his stomach. He swallowed hard. "Is she—" He stood and staggered from where he sat with the family by the lake. They watched him with worry and question.

"She'll be okay. She has a broken arm, and her knee and face are messed up."

"Is the baby okay?" Panic raced through every inch of him. Nerves wound tight like a rubber band on a toy airplane propeller. Dinner worked its way up his esophagus.

"I don't know. They didn't say anything, and I didn't even think to ask."

"You knew about the baby, right?" He walked to the tree line.

"Yes, she told us last night. Let me find out, and I'll call you back."

"Wait! Margaret, where is she? What hospital?"

"Hennepin County Medical Center. I'll call you back as soon as I find out. Josef, she's okay so drive carefully. There's no need to rush. Okay?"

"I hear you. I'll be leaving shortly. I'm at my parent's in North Branch, so it shouldn't take too long. I'll be waiting to hear from you." Josef hung up, bent over and threw up into the hostas.

His mother stepped to his side and rubbed his back. "We heard and figured out what we didn't hear. Will you be okay to drive? One of us can take you."

He spit to clear his mouth and stood. "Sorry about your plants. I'll be fine, but can I leave Blondie here?"

"Of course. And don't worry about the plants. Hostas are hearty. So is Catherine." They approached the family who stood in a worried circle.

"Cat was in an accident and is hurt but okay." His eyes filled with tears, and he fell into a chair. "I don't know about the baby." He cried and let his mother comfort him.

Barbara stroked his back, "Let it out, honey. Let it out."

"Josef," Maureen spoke softly and squatted in front of him. "I don't know the situation, but I do know that at this early on in the stage of pregnancy, chances are really good for the baby. I'll be praying for them both."

"Thanks." He sniffled. "That means a lot." He allowed himself to cry a few moments then stopped because he had to be there for her. "I'll keep ya posted."

After receiving hugs from everyone, he punched the destination into his navigation system and left for Minneapolis. Fifteen minutes on the road, his phone rang.

"Josef, the baby is fine. They had to ask if she could be pregnant prior to taking x-rays."

"Thank God. Thank you for finding out and letting me know."

"They ran a blood test and her HCG level was over nine thousand. She'll need to go to her doctor in about a week to make sure the level is either the same or higher."

"What if it isn't?"

"She could be losing the baby. But they did an ultrasound, and everything was good from what they could see. With her only being close to three weeks, they can't get a heartbeat yet. They don't foresee any reason why the number shouldn't go up."

"Is Cat awake? Can I talk to her?"

"Yes, but I'm not in the room. She's shaken up and in pain. Listen, I need go. The doctor's coming. Please try not to worry while you're driving. Save it for when you get here. She's okay."

"How can you be so calm?" He didn't understand how she could remain sane.

"I'm not as calm as you think. I'll see you when you get here."

He hung up and focused on the road he drove on and the road his life traveled. Knowing the baby was okay helped ease some of the tension, but not knowing the details of the accident and Cat's condition ate at him. He'd be by her side soon enough.

The phone rang ten minutes later, and he answered.

"Hi, Josef."

"Margaret! Is everything okay?"

"Fine. Everything is fine. They're releasing Catherine. Why don't you go straight to our place, and we'll meet you there."

"Okay, I'll see you there."

Cat and her family hadn't come home yet when Josef arrived so he waited in his truck at the curb. The sound of every passing car had his heart pounding against his chest, adding to the anxiety. They pulled into the driveway, and he immediately exited the pickup. He swallowed hard. His jaw clenched at the sight of her.

Catherine's left arm was casted, and her face was bloodied and bruised.

"Josef, she's going to be fine." Margaret stepped beside him and paused. "I have the ring. They had to cut it off because of the swelling."

"I don't care about the damned ring. What the hell happened?" He spoke in a harsh growl as his hands curled into tight-fisted balls.

"Let's go inside first. I'm sure she'd like to get into bed."

"I'll carry you in." Josef scooped her into his arms and carefully backed her out of the car. Mike held the front door open, and Josef walked straight up the stairs to her room.

"I don't want to go to sleep." Cat stated, groggy in a drugged state.

"You're more tired than you think." He sat her on the bed.

"Catherine," Margaret came into the room. "Let's get you out of those clothes and into something more comfortable."

"I'll be downstairs." He left the women alone. Her mother would get Cat to stay in bed.

"Would you like something to drink?" Mike asked from the kitchen as he came down the stairs. "Beer, scotch, whiskey?"

"I'll take a shot of scotch. I promised Cat I wouldn't drink during the pregnancy, but this warrants a shot of something. Shit. What happened, Mike?" His hands shook so he shoved them into his pockets.

"She was on I-35 W coming through the downtown area and a semi hit a car, starting a chain reaction which sent her spinning," Mike explained while pouring two shots. "The pickup ended up backwards and slammed into the side wall. One person died at the scene. Another is in critical condition, and several others were hurt. They don't know what caused the semi driver to lose control, but are investigating. Here you go." He handed Josef the scotch.

The two men threw back their glasses and swallowed.

"Ah, good shit."

"Thanks." Josef set the glass down. "What about the dogs? She had all three with her." The dogs meant the world to her along with any other living creature.

"Fuzzy didn't make it. Darby's two hind legs are broken, and Fritz broke the hind leg she just fixed. They both got cut up but will be fine. They were taken to the Humane Society."

"Damn!" Josef knew Cat would have a hard time with this news. "I'd like to bring them back to my place when they're okay to go."

"That'd help her and us out. Margaret's going to bring the cats here and will arrange for someone to take care of the horses."

"I'll take one of those," Margaret said, entering the room. "Here's the engagement ring."

She placed the ring in Josef's shaking hand. "Thank you."

"I'm happy to see you two have worked through your differences," she said.

"I want to marry her as soon as possible." He stared at the ring. "I don't want to wait until after she's fully recovered or after the baby's been born. We can do the big thing later if that's what she wants."

"What do you want me to do?" She threw back the amber liquid and slowly swallowed.

"Father Tim from St. Michael's won't marry us. Can you check with your priest? And could we get married at your house?"

"Of course, on both accounts. If for some reason our priest won't marry you, would you like me to arrange for a judge to preside over the ceremony?"

"That would be great. I'm going up to see her."

At her bedside, he held her left hand in his palm, resting the other hand over hers. Knowing she and the baby were both okay, he decided to wait to tell her about her beloved pets. She was so groggy she hadn't thought to ask. But he knew a body could handle only so much trauma. Cat had had enough for one day.

"I'm sorry," she croaked between dry lips. Her tongue darted out to moisten them but failed. "The baby?" Her speech came slow, sad pleading eyes watching him.

"The baby's fine. You're beat up but will be okay, too." He gently massaged the fingers in his hands. Tears moistened his eyes and slid down his cheeks. "I want us to get married as soon as you're able to. I love you." His head resting on the bed, the tears flowed. He almost lost her.

"I'd like that." The words were slow and spaced as she worked past the dryness in her mouth and throat. "I love you."

* * * *

Three weeks after the accident, Catherine slipped the simple white satin, floor length, tank sheath over her head. Her mother pulled the smooth soft fabric over her chest and hips. Today she was going to marry Josef, the man she once loved and let go. The man she found love with again.

This time she wasn't letting him go.

"You look beautiful," her mother said. "But I wouldn't expect anything different."

A knock at the door and her father asked, "Are you ready?"

Her mother opened the door, and her father's eyes moistened.

"Dad, don't start that. I can't afford to mess up my make-up."

Her father dabbed his eyes dry. "You look stunning. Let's get you to the altar."

Down the short flight of stairs and at the patio door, her mother handed her the small bouquet, kissed her cheek, walked the short distance to the front row chairs and sat.

Soft music played as Catherine and her father slowly approached Josef waiting at the end of the aisle. Close immediate family filled white chairs. Josef wore a pair of khaki pants and a black linen shirt. His eyes, moist with joy, and his face with a broad smile left her reeling with unfettered joy.

The priest from her parent's church stood before them and performed the short-sweet-just-what-her-body-ordered ceremony.

Father announced, "You may kiss the bride."

Josef held her by the waist, kissed her passionately and scooped her into his arms. She squealed, and he quieted her with a kiss, receiving cheers from both families. He then carried her to her bedroom. He gently placed her on the bed and delivered a kiss. Joining her on the mattress, he guided her to her back. "I love you, Mrs. Garrison."

Epilogue

Catherine's parents had arrived last night to help with the Thanksgiving Day feast. Today their house would be filled with both of their families. She didn't know how everyone was going to fit in the large house. Josef assured her there was plenty of space for everyone.

Cinnamon. Catherine inhaled. Mom's cinnamon rolls. Soft voices amid the clattering of pots drifted up the stairwell and through the vents. A hint of the sun rising broke through the slates of the bedroom window shades. She rolled to her back with the five-month baby bump tenting the covers and glanced at Josef, hoping she didn't wake him.

"I was wondering when you were going to wake up." He laid his hand on her belly, and the warmth seeped through her thin tee shirt.

"How long have you been awake?" Her hand covered his, and the baby kicked.

"Whoa! Good morning, little one." He rubbed Catherine's belly and earned another kick. "Not long. Are you ready to leave in the morning?"

"I'm more than ready for our honeymoon." She kissed him.

"Can I help with the horses today?"

"Your help is welcome anytime. First I want one of those cinnamon rolls, then we can take care of the horses before getting ready for our guest and the main event." Her legs swung out and over the edge of the bed as she sat up.

"My mom said they'd be here around nine. She didn't want your mom doing all the work."

"Mom's looking forward to seeing everyone," she stated and walked into the bathroom.

Josef had his work clothes on when they passed each other in the bathroom a few minutes later. "I'll meet you in the kitchen." She pecked him on the cheek.

Walking through the hall, she smoothed the maternity blouse over her belly. "The cinnamon rolls smell delicious," Catherine said when she entered the spacious kitchen.

"Well, good morning to you, too. How's my little grandbaby doing?"

"Just fine, Mom. Or should I say Grandma." The two women laughed. "Joseph said his parents would be here around nine. We're going to eat a cinnamon roll, take care of the horses and will be back to get ready and help." Catherine went to the cupboard to retrieve two small plates.

"You just take it easy today, dear. Barbara and I will take care of everything."

"I'll take it easy, but I'm not going to sit back and watch the two of you do all the work. Now where are those delicious rolls?" With two large cinnamon rolls dished up, she set the plates on the kitchen table.

"Have you and Josef thought of names for the baby yet?"

"Yeah, Mrs. Garrison, have you come up with any names?" Josef winked at Catherine as he entered the room. This discussion came up frequently between them.

"I'm not saying anything." Catherine poured two cups of coffee. Since her pregnancy, she allowed herself only one cup of coffee a day.

"The rolls smell delicious, Margaret. Thank you." He gave her a kiss on the cheek as she worked with the enormous turkey.

"So you *have* given some thought to names?" Her mom asked, not missing the clue that Catherine had some ideas.

Catherine ignored her in favor of her mom's fabulous cinnamon roll.

After breakfast, they crossed the road, and she smiled at the small sign stating Fuller-Garrison Farm. A large carved wood sign down by the new barn announced—Four Hooves and Paws Rescue. A gift from Josef, the sign brought happiness to her life every day.

She and Joseph worked as a team, mucking and feeding the horses. Of the four rescue horses, two remained. The new owners of Warren's farm had purchased Rusty and Steel. At the first of the month, Magnolia was purchased as a Christmas present for a young girl. Magnolia would remain on the farm with Churchill as the new owners needed a temporary home for her.

The horses taken care of, Catherine strolled to the concrete bench Joseph surprised her with after moving to the farm. The bench meant everything to her. He had used the cinderblocks from the original barn for the foundation of the bench and wood slats from the old barn formed the seat.

A large portion of the original farmhouse basement was dismantled for safety reasons, since the tornado left a large hole in the ground. Josef removed two of the stonewalls, the front of the house and the stairwell, moving earth and changing the landscape so the rock walls of the basement stood as a retaining wall. This was where her bench sat. In a place she once hated to venture. Now a place that brought solace.

Fluffy, the only kitten to survive the tornado, strolled by their feet, stopped and rubbed against Cat's shins. Josef sat beside Cat in silence for several moments.

"If we have a girl, I'd like to name her Elaine Elizabeth." Catherine leaned into him. "If we have a boy I'd like to name him Jacob Gustav after his great-grandfathers."

"I couldn't agree more."

Josef folded her in the cocoon of his embrace as a breeze caressed Catherine's shoulder. *Elaine.* The baby gently kicked, and Catherine knew—they would have a little girl named Elaine.

About the Author

Born and raised in Minnesota, Jody remains close to home, living with her husband of more than twenty years as well as three children and a cat named Holly. Growing up, she enjoyed reading V.C. Andrews' Dollanganger series, S.E. Hinton and Stephen King to name a few.

She's traveled throughout the United States, to the Bahamas and Cancun, Mexico. Between watching soccer games, scrapbooking and being the COO of the Vitek household, she writes contemporary romances.

You can find Jody on Facebook: Jody Vitek Author, on Twitter: @JodyVitek and you can email her at: info@jodyvitek.com

Other Works by the author with Melange Books, LLC

Florida Heat